Carrickstowe

N

Tregower
Hamlet

Westward
Beach

Pendragon
Manor

SOUT
MOOR

CASTLE
KEY

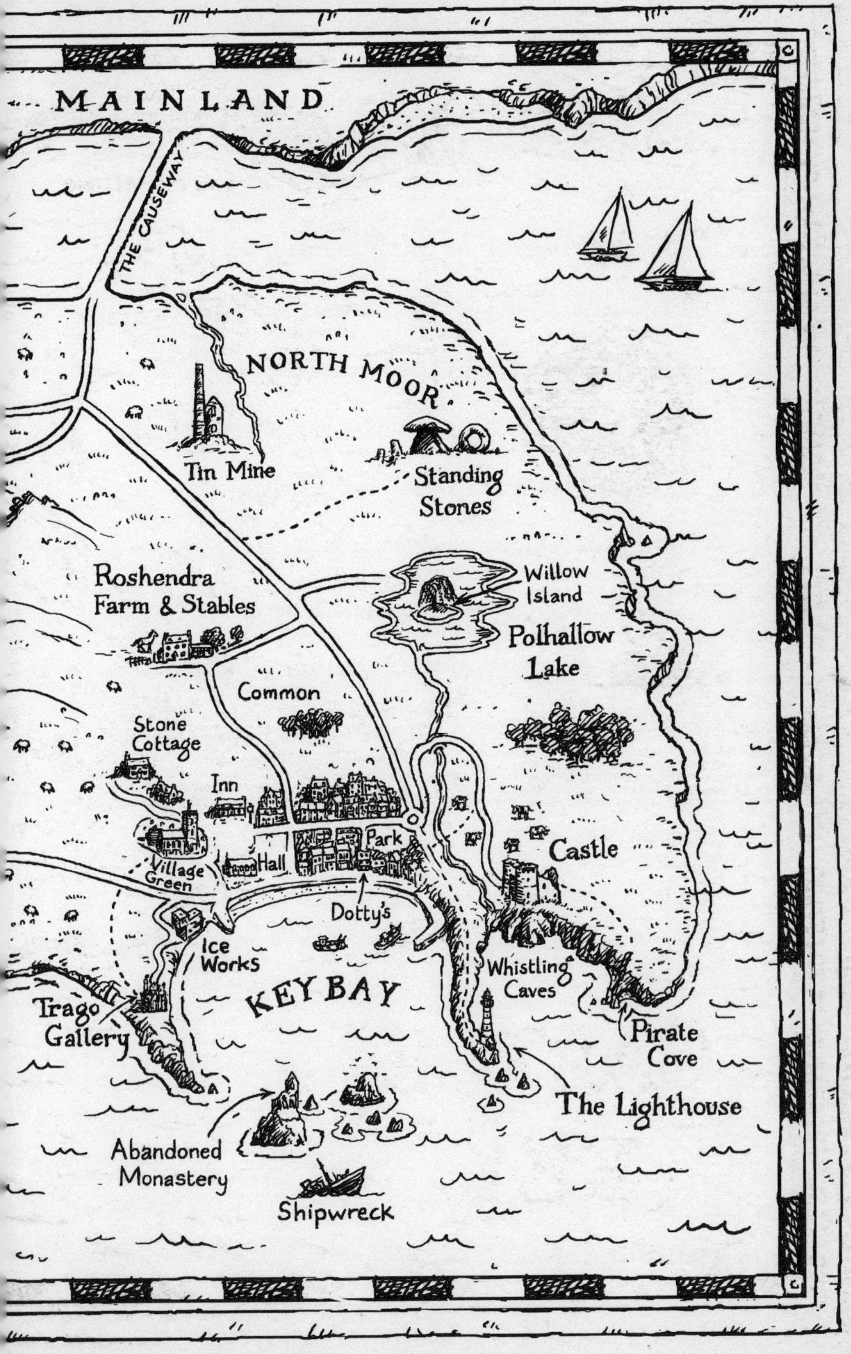

MAINLAND

THE CAUSEWAY

NORTH MOOR

Tin Mine

Standing
Stones

Roshendra
Farm & Stables

Willow
Island

Polhallow
Lake

Common

Stone
Cottage

Inn

Castle

Village
Green

Hall

Park

Dotty's

Ice
Works

KEY BAY

Whistling
Caves

Trago
Gallery

Pirate
Cove

The Lighthouse

Abandoned
Monastery

Shipwreck

Collect all the Adventure Island *books*

ADVENTURE ISLAND

THE MYSTERY OF THE MISSING MASTERPIECE

Helen Moss

Illustrated by Leo Hartas

Orion
Children's Books

First published in Great Britain in 2011
by Orion Children's Books
a division of the Orion Publishing Group Ltd
Orion House
5 Upper St Martin's Lane
London WC2H 9EA
An Hachette UK company

3 5 7 9 10 8 6 4

A catalogue record for this book is
available from the British Library.

ISBN 978 1 4440 0331 4

Printed in Great Britain by Clays Ltd, St Ives plc

For Ed and Will

One

The Great Fête Riot

'*And the first prize goes to Emily Wild and Drift!*'
The crackly PA system could hardly be heard over the roars of the crowd.

Scott and Jack cheered and whistled. In the ring, Emily knelt down and buried her face in her little dog's soft fur.

Drift sat proudly as the mayor pinned a red rosette to his collar. His ears popped up in an expression of

9

Eager Excitement; the black one pointing at the sky, taking in the applause, the white one with brown spots tucked back towards Emily, in case she had further instructions. He was feeling extraordinarily pleased with himself. They'd just aced the Obedience Trial in the dog show at the Castle Key summer fête for the third year running. And they'd left the competition standing – not to mention sitting, begging and rolling over. Drift trotted round with Emily in a lap of honour, as if he'd won Supreme Champion at Crufts.

Emily high-fived with Scott and Jack as she came out of the show ring. She was pretty stoked with the victory too. The Obedience Trial had been a walkover. Drift could churn out Heel, Stay and Fetch in his sleep. Emily had also taught him a range of commands more suited to an Undercover Agent's Right Hand Dog, of course, such as Stake Out and Lookout Duty.

'Entering Drift in the Obedience Trial is like playing Wayne Rooney in the school under sevens football team,' Scott laughed. 'No one else stands a chance.'

'Did you see that border collie that kept trying to cut in front and put us off?' Emily asked.

'Yeah,' Jack said. 'We were about to make an official complaint!'

'So what does Drift have up his sleeve next?' Scott asked. 'Brain surgery? Synchronized swimming?'

Emily laughed. 'We're working on this brilliant new command called Distraction. We'll show you when it's ready. Right now, let's find something to drink. Being champions is thirsty work!'

Drift panted in agreement.

'The refreshment tent's over there,' Jack said. 'I just happened to notice they have some pretty awesome cakes.'

Scott rolled his eyes. 'Why am I not surprised?' Jack could detect a single cake crumb, the way sharks could detect a drop of blood in the ocean.

Scott had to admit that this whole village fête experience was turning out to be a lot more fun than he'd expected. He'd only really come to humour Emily – and to cheer Drift on in the dog show, of course. True, the lucky dip, the plant stall and Guess the Name of the Teddy Bear didn't exactly have the thrills and spills of a day out at Alton Towers, and the most extreme ride of the day was a gentle stroll round the green on a donkey, but the fête did have *some* things going for it, like the coconut shy (Scott had won five times) and the sight of Colin Warnock, the curate, dashing around with his video camera. He was taking his filming as seriously as if he were directing a new Star Wars movie.

Inside the marquee in the centre of the green, a long trestle table was crammed with cakes and cookies of every kind. 'We'd better pick three each and share them,' Jack said. 'Or maybe *four* to be on the safe side?'

The friends sat down with drinks and cakes and a bowl of water for Drift. At the next table, an artist had set up an easel and was sketching portraits. Scott recognized Mrs Roberts, their next-door neighbour in Church Lane. At least, she was *Aunt Kate's* next-door neighbour. The boys were staying with their great-aunt for the summer while their dad was away on an archaeological dig in Africa. Scott couldn't help laughing at himself when he realized he was actually starting to think of Stone Cottage as *home.* He'd never have believed *that* could happen when they'd first arrived from London just a few short weeks ago.

Mrs Roberts smiled shyly behind her large glasses and waved to the friends. A small mousy lady with neat, straight black hair in a bun, she didn't fit Scott's image of an artist. Artists should look more, well, *artistic.* More like Emily's mum, for example, who was all floaty kaftans and mad hair pinned up with paintbrushes.

'Mrs Roberts used to be my art teacher when I was at primary school,' Emily explained. 'She's really nice. You know the blonde girl who's helping Vicky White with the donkey rides? That's her daughter, Laura. She's working at the riding stables at Roshendra Farm for the summer.'

Jack snagged a cup from the next table and pretended to peer at the tea leaves. He nudged Emily's elbow and laughed through his mouthful of chocolate cake. 'Ah, yes, what do we have here?' he cackled, doing his best gypsy fortune-teller impression. 'Scott will suddenly develop a burning interest in horse-riding!' He reverted to his own voice. 'You can tell by the way he was looking at the lovely Laura. *Ow!*' he added as Scott's trainer made contact with his shin under the table.

Emily had got used to ignoring the boys' scuffles. 'So what are we going to do next?' she asked.

'Let's ask Mrs Roberts to do a picture of Jack,' Scott said. 'Then again,' he added, 'drawing his ugly mug would probably break her paintbrush or something!'

There were more kicks under the table. Emily sighed. The boys were great fun. They were usually brave and sometimes smart, and they could both be pretty useful in a crisis, but neither of them had the ability to plan beyond the next five minutes. 'I didn't mean *now*. I meant, what's our next *investigation* going to be?' It felt like light years since they'd found a treasure map and a chest of hidden gold, even though she was still limping slightly from the sprained ankle she'd picked up on Gulliver's Island. But she was already on the lookout for a new case to solve.

Jack looked around the tent as if a fully-fledged mystery might be hiding behind a tea urn. Since they'd arrived in Castle Key and made friends with Emily, they'd had some awesome adventures. But things *had* gone a bit quiet lately.

'I was talking to Mrs Loveday at the cake table and she told me there was a major kerfuffle in the Vegetable Competition this morning,' Scott suggested. 'We could investigate that. Someone accused Old Bob of bribing

13

the judges to award his onions Best in Show.'

'Oooh, *controversial*!' Jack laughed.

'I am *not*,' Emily stated firmly, 'embarking upon an investigation named Operation Onion – however controversial it may be!'

Jack snorted. Coke bubbles spurted out of his nose.

'Well, we can't just order a mystery on the internet,' Scott laughed. 'We'll have to keep our eyes open and be patient.' He grinned at his brother. Emily wasn't exactly known for her patience! Then again, nor was Jack. Scott began to hum *Whatever Will Be, Will Be* just to wind them both up. But he stopped mid-hum as the marquee was suddenly transformed into a tornado of smashing plates, ripping canvas and pounding hooves.

'What?' Scott spluttered, springing out of his chair.

A wild-eyed donkey trailing strings of red, white and blue bunting stampeded past. It was followed by Vicky White and Laura Roberts. '*Wallace! Stop!*' they screamed. But Wallace was in no mood to stop. He buckarooed his way across the tent, scattering tables and chairs and cups and saucers in his path, until he reached Mrs Roberts' easel and head-butted it into the air. Meanwhile, a second braying donkey careened onto the scene, heading straight for the cake table. People fled in every direction. 'The starter gun for the children's sack race spooked them!' Vicky shouted.

'*Gromit! No!*' Laura yelled as the donkey's hooves slammed down on one end of the cake table, flipping the other end up like a giant see-saw.

A barrage of Victoria sponges, chocolate brownies, fairy cakes and flapjacks rained down. Buttercream bombs pelted Mrs Roberts' easel and meringue missiles spattered the vicar's cassock. Glacé cherries and walnuts sprayed the tent like machine-gun fire. Drift was having a lovely time licking whipped cream and strawberry icing off the grass.

Emily nudged Scott and pointed at Colin Warnock. The curate was still filming, in spite of the chocolate sprinkles stuck to his crest of purple hair.

There's nothing mysterious about a pair of crazed donkeys running amok in a cake tent, Scott thought, *but it's certainly livened things up a bit!*

'I'm covered from head to foot in cake!' Jack shouted, throwing out his arms. 'Have I died and gone to heaven?'

Two

Technophobia

The next morning was cloudy and grey. Jack and Scott lingered at the kitchen table long after they'd finished their bacon and eggs. Jack sighed and tapped his fingers on the table. What to do in Castle Key on an overcast Sunday morning? In London he could give his mates a call and see what was on at the cinema. If they wanted to catch a film *here*, they'd have to go to Carrickstowe – and he couldn't be bothered to cycle across the causeway to the mainland.

Emily was right. They really *did* need a new investigation.

Aunt Kate was reading the Sunday paper. She turned a page, tucked a wisp of white hair into a hairgrip and poured herself another cup of tea. Scott reached for his fancy new mobile phone. Jack grinned. If it was possible to *marry* a phone, there'd have been wedding bells by now. Scott had bought it with his share of the reward money for recovering the hidden gold on Gulliver's Island. He could spend hours downloading music and apps, and watching YouTube videos.

Jack yawned and rolled pieces of bread into little balls. Aunt Kate looked at him over her glasses and offered him a section of her paper. Jack shook his head. He'd already read the sports pages. He was going to be reduced to reading the fashion supplement if *something* didn't happen soon. He was lining up a bread pellet to flick at Scott's ear, when Scott suddenly roared with laughter. He sprawled back in his chair, holding his phone out in front of him.

'What?' Jack craned his neck to see the small screen. Scott was always making out he'd just seen the most hilarious video ever, and then not letting Jack see it. It was probably only a cat playing the piano anyway!

But, for once, his brother seemed keen to share.

'Look at this,' Scott laughed. 'We're internet superstars! Donkey Demolition at Castle Key Fête!'

He turned the sound up and passed the phone to Jack. 'Colin Warnock must have posted it.'

It was all there in the clip. Wallace upending Mrs Roberts' easel, Gromit sending the cake table into orbit, Laura and Vicky trying to capture the marauding donkeys. Jack even caught a glimpse of himself, Scott and Emily, leaping up from their table to escape the cake-storm.

'Awesome!' Jack whistled. 'We've made it into the top ten most viewed clips! Castle Key has never been so famous!'

Scott handed the phone across the table to Aunt Kate. 'Oh, dear! Just look at the vicar's expression!' she laughed. 'I think he might have swallowed a whole macaroon!' Aunt Kate was still chuckling as she folded her paper and began clearing the table. 'Why don't you boys pop next door and show that video to Mrs Roberts? She and Laura have starring roles!'

Scott nodded. It wasn't as if they had anything better to do. 'I'll text Emily and she can come with us. I wonder if she's seen this yet.'

—

When Scott, Jack and Emily rang the doorbell of Lilac Cottage they were greeted by a frenzy of high-pitched barking. A little white terrier shot out of the door, bouncing up and down like a flea on a trampoline. Drift wagged his tail and sniffed politely.

'Sorry,' Mrs Roberts laughed. 'Biscuit's always like this when anyone comes to the house. Take no notice! Come on in.'

Emily hadn't been inside before and was surprised to find that although the outside of the cottage looked as traditional as all the others in Church Lane, with its stone walls and slate roof and hanging baskets of geraniums, the inside was a different matter. The wooden floorboards and beams had been stripped to a pale dried-grass colour and the walls were all whitewashed. The furniture was sleek and modern and there were blinds instead of curtains at the windows. It looked like an advert for a range of expensive Swedish sofas, and not at all what you'd expect from Mrs Roberts' rather frumpy appearance.

'How are you getting on at Carrickstowe High?' Mrs Roberts asked Emily. 'You were always good at art. Very vivid imagination.'

While they chatted over lemonade and biscuits, Emily looked around the room, memorizing every detail – as she always did when she entered a new location. You never knew when keen observation would be the key to an investigation! There were shelves full of art books and the white walls were dotted with prints of famous paintings. Emily recognized a vase of sunflowers by Van Gogh and some hazy Impressionist pictures of water lilies and riverbanks. The picture hanging above the fireplace looked a bit like the Mona Lisa, although the lady was wearing a blue dress and holding a lamb on her knee. It was like being in a miniature art gallery. When they'd finished their drinks Mrs Roberts showed them her studio in the conservatory. It looked out over the back garden, where Drift and Biscuit were playing a boisterous game of Chase the Tail. Canvases were propped against the wall and there were jars of brushes on the windowsills. A half-finished painting of a little girl in a flower meadow was clipped onto the easel.

'That's pretty,' Emily said.

Mrs Roberts smiled. 'Thank you. It's for Laura's room. A surprise for when she comes back.'

'Comes back?' Emily asked.

'Don't look so worried,' Mrs Roberts laughed. 'She's staying with Vicky at Roshendra Farm for a few weeks. She has so many early starts at the riding stables.'

They went back into the living room and sat down. 'Now, what was it you wanted to show me?' Mrs Roberts asked.

'It's a video clip of the fête,' Scott explained. 'When the donkeys went bonkers in the cake tent. It's got you and Laura in it.' He pressed play and handed Mrs Roberts his phone.

Mrs Roberts adjusted her glasses and held the phone gingerly on her lap.

'It's dead popular,' Jack said. 'Look, it's been seen all over the world!' He leaned across and scrolled down to show Mrs Roberts. 'There're comments here from Brazil and Australia and everywhere.'

Mrs Roberts stared at the screen and nodded slowly. Her smile had vanished and she bit the inside of her cheek. Emily noticed her hand trembling as she returned the phone to Scott. 'Yes, that's very funny!' she said in a brittle voice. 'Now, if you'll excuse me, I do have a lot of work to get on with . . .'

—

'That was well weird!' Jack said as they closed the front gate of Lilac Cottage behind them. 'The way she looked at that phone, it was like we'd passed her a live hand grenade!'

'Mrs Roberts obviously has *technophobia*!' Scott said knowledgeably. 'Some older people are freaked out by modern technology.'

'Hmm,' Emily murmured. She'd seen the fear behind Mrs Roberts' glasses too. But whatever her old art teacher was afraid of, Emily was pretty sure it wasn't Scott's phone, even if it *was* the latest model.

Mrs Roberts *had* run the lunchtime computer club at school, after all.

Emily's *vivid imagination* was working overtime already.

Three

Operation Break-in

When Scott and Jack met Emily at Dotty's Tea Rooms the following morning they had some exciting news to report. Actually, Scott thought, it would probably only score about a three point five on the ten-point International Excitement Scale, but it was better than nothing.

'What?' Emily asked impatiently, as they took their drinks to an outside table with a view across the harbour and the bay beyond. Although still overcast, the weather was very hot. In fact, *hot* was an understatement. It was like sitting under a giant hairdryer. Even the seagulls were wilting. From the evil-looking purple clouds lurking on the horizon, it was clear a storm was brewing.

'Mrs Roberts has had a break-in!' Scott announced.

Jack took a bite of his white chocolate and pecan muffin. 'Yeah. A *burglary*!'

Scott rolled his eyes. 'I think Em could've figured out it was a burglary all by herself! People don't just break in, have a cup of tea, then wander off again, do they?'

Emily ignored the boys' quarrel and pulled her notebook out of her bag. 'OK, give me the details.'

Scott shrugged. 'A policewoman just came round this morning and said someone had broken into Lilac Cottage during the night. She warned Aunt Kate to make sure she locks up properly in case the burglar's still in the area.'

Emily chewed the end of her pen. 'Mode of entry to premises?'

'Dunno,' Jack said.

'What was taken?'

'Not sure,' Scott admitted.

Emily shook her head in disbelief. 'Time of break-in?'

'Unknown!' Jack felt like a contestant on *The Weakest Link* – and he had a feeling he wasn't winning any prizes.

Emily closed her notebook with a weary sigh. 'The break-in happened next door to Stone Cottage. Your bedroom window is metres away from the scene of the crime. Didn't you hear *anything*?'

Jack and Scott looked at each other sheepishly over their Cokes.

'Well, I'm sure *I* would have noticed if *my* next-door neighbour was being burgled!' Emily said.

Scott snorted. 'Em, you live in a lighthouse on the end of a promontory sticking out into the sea. The only neighbours you have are seagulls!'

Jack made a serious face and shook his head. 'Well, you have to watch those gulls! Dodgy characters! Always breaking into each others' nests, nicking bits of old fish.'

Scott laughed. Knowing Emily, he wouldn't be surprised if she *did* have her binoculars on standby to keep tabs on the gulls.

Emily tossed her long chocolate-brown curls and stuck out her chin. 'So, are we investigating this crime or not?'

Jack watched a fishing trawler chugging out to sea. He could see the hazy outline of Gulliver's Island in the distance. 'It's just a boring old burglary. It's not exactly in the same league as buried gold . . .'

'Or rescuing a famous film star who's been kidnapped by a ghost,' Scott added, remembering their other adventures. 'Or Saxon treasure stashed in the Whistling Caves . . .'

'Alright, alright!' Emily held up her hands. 'But it's not as if we've got a waiting list of Magnificent Mysteries on the books either!'

'Yeah, that's true. I'm in!' Jack said, draining the last of his Coke.

Scott opened Emily's notebook at a new page and put her pen in her hand. 'Go on! I know you're dying to.'

Emily grinned. *OPERATION BREAK-IN*, she wrote. Then she took her ruler and underlined it twice.

—

'The police don't hold out much hope of catching the thieves,' Mrs Roberts said as she sank down onto her sofa and smoothed her shapeless brown skirt over her knees. 'I don't want to make a fuss.'

The friends had called at Lilac Cottage with the excuse of offering to take Biscuit for a walk in case Mrs Roberts was too upset to go out. Surprisingly though, she didn't seem as shaken by the break-in as Emily had expected.

'*We* could investigate the burglary for you,' Emily offered.

Mrs Roberts smiled. 'Thank you, dear, but I don't think there's much to investigate. It's just one of those things.'

'We won't get in the way,' Emily coaxed.

Mrs Roberts closed her eyes as if she didn't have

the energy to object any more. Jack knew *that* feeling. Emily didn't give up easily!

Emily pulled out her notebook. 'I just need to ask a few questions. How did the burglars effect their entry?'

Mrs Roberts frowned. 'Er, sorry?'

'She means how did they get in,' Scott explained.

'Through the window in my studio,' Mrs Roberts said. 'I heard a noise and came downstairs. The window was open but they'd already gone. The catch is a bit stiff and I probably hadn't closed it properly.'

Emily nodded. 'And can you give me a list of what was taken?'

'Just some cash from the kitchen drawer. And some of the pictures, of course.' Mrs Roberts pointed up at the rectangular patches of lighter paint on the walls. 'They've taken three or four. The van Gogh sunflowers. A Picasso.'

'And the one from above the fireplace?' Emily prompted. 'The woman with the sheep.'

Mrs Roberts glanced at the empty space on the wall. 'That's right. That was Leonardo da Vinci's *Lady in Blue.*'

Jack whistled. 'How much was that lot worth?'

Mrs Roberts smiled. 'Oh, they were just cheap prints! They weren't worth anything at all, really. The burglars will be very disappointed.'

Jack was disappointed too. If the burglars had got away with a priceless work of art or two that would've spiced up Operation Break-in no end!

Emily made a list of the missing items in her notebook. 'Do you know of anyone who might have a grudge against you?' she asked. 'Any enemies?'

Jack tried to disguise his snort of laughter as a cough. Sometimes Emily cracked him up with her Chief Inspector act! *Enemies?* Mrs Roberts was an art teacher in a village primary school on a little Cornish island. What *enemies* could she possibly have? A six-year-old who'd been scarred for life by a nasty finger-painting accident? A teacher who'd caught Mrs Roberts drinking out of their favourite coffee mug in the staff room?

But to his astonishment, Mrs Roberts didn't roll around in her chair with laughter. 'No! Of course not!' she gasped, her hand fluttering nervously to her throat. 'Why ever would you think such a thing?'

'I'm *sorry*, Mrs Roberts,' Scott said in a soothing voice, shooting Emily a warning look. 'We didn't mean to upset you. We'll take Biscuit for that walk now, shall we?'

'We need a good Observation Post for keeping watch on Lilac Cottage,' Emily said. They'd taken Biscuit home to Mrs Roberts after a run-around on the beach and a cooling splash in the waves with Drift. Now the friends were in the back garden of Stone Cottage. 'I have a weird feeling about this break-in,' Emily went on. 'Why didn't the burglars take the telly or anything?

And why doesn't Mrs Roberts seem to want to catch the burglars? She looked *terrible*. It could just be the heat, I suppose, but I'm sure there's more to this than meets the eye!'

'Like Mrs Roberts' vast hoards of *sworn enemies,* you mean?' Jack joked.

But Scott agreed with Emily. 'What I can't figure out is why the burglars only targeted Lilac Cottage. It doesn't look any different from the other houses in Church Lane. And I know Aunt Kate leaves half her windows open downstairs.'

'There's something else fishy about it,' Emily said, twisting a long curl round her finger. 'Something that keeps nagging at the back of my mind, but I can't work out exactly what it is.'

Jack shrugged. He couldn't understand why the other two were getting all mysterious about a burglary. It was just your basic break-in. He left them to get on with spooking each other out and wandered over to an enormous chestnut tree. *You'd get a great view of the back of Lilac Cottage from up there*, he thought. He was inspecting the branches for climb-ability when he noticed a bit of old rope hanging down from the thick foliage. He gave it a little tug. 'Ouch!' he yelped as a stick landed on his head. The stick was attached to more rope and tied up with other sticks. Jack teased the tangle apart. *It was a rope ladder!*

Jack looked round for Scott and Emily but they were

busy scoping for potential hideouts under the laurel bushes. *I'll check this out on my own first,* he thought.

Climbing the rope ladder was hard work. It lurched back and forth with every step. At last he came to a platform of wooden planks nailed across the branches. He hauled himself up through a hole in the platform and found himself in a tree house. It was smothered with bird droppings and cobwebs, but it had walls and a roof and everything and it was shaded from the scorching sun. 'Cool!' Jack breathed. He couldn't believe they hadn't discovered it before.

An old book was lying splay-paged among dead leaves under an abandoned bird's nest in the corner. *How awesome would it be if I found* another *treasure map?* His heart doing wheelies with excitement, Jack picked up the crusty old book and brushed away the grime. *DR WHO ANNUAL, 1979!* Jack laughed. *Oh well*, he thought, *two treasure maps in one summer would've been asking too much!* But 1979? That was practically *prehistoric*! The tree house must have been built by Dad and his brother Tim, when *they* used to come and stay with Aunt Kate. Jack turned and peeped out through the branches. *Result!* A perfect squirrel's-eye view of Lilac Cottage!

He couldn't wait to tell Scott and Emily he'd found the new headquarters for Operation Break-in!

Four

A Mysterious Arrival

The friends lost no time in kitting out the tree house as a fully operational HQ. First, they made a pulley system to hoist Drift up to the platform. He thoroughly approved of this new mode of transport, and sat upright in the basket – his spotted ear twitching with excitement – as he was hauled up on a rope. The next job was to clean, patch up a few holes and install the surveillance equipment: old cushions, bottles of water, several packets of biscuits and Emily's spare binoculars. Then they settled down to watch.

Jack wasn't sure what they were watching *for*.

'Criminals *always* return to the scene of the crime,' Emily stated confidently.

Jack thought that was rubbish. He was quite sure bank robbers didn't pop back into the bank the next day to have another look around. But he let it go.

After an hour, even Emily had to concede that nothing was happening at Lilac Cottage – apart from Biscuit barking at a cat, a flock of sparrows landing on the bird table and the postman dropping off a parcel. And she still couldn't pin down that nagging *something* that was hovering just out of reach in the corner of her mind. So when she spotted Mrs Roberts heading off down Church Lane with her shopping basket, she decided on a change of plan.

'We need to do a Crime Scene Analysis,' she announced. Drift hopped into his basket and moments later they were all climbing over the fence into the next-door garden.

'Nice roses!' Jack said, as they stood pondering the flowerbed beneath Mrs Roberts' studio window.

'Get back!' Emily cried. 'You'll contaminate the evidence!' She was kneeling on the grass with her head among the rose stems. 'Footprint!' she cried, whipping a tape measure out of her bag. She made a note of the measurements and took photographs with her phone.

'And, what's this?' Emily pounced on a small object and held it up.

'A cigarette end?' Jack ventured, hoping it wasn't a trick question.

'Exactly!' Emily's dark eyes held a glint of triumph. '*Someone* has been loitering outside this window. And those scuff marks in the soil could have been made by a ladder! We're onto something here!'

Jack grinned. 'Yeah, the window-cleaner! He called at Stone Cottage the other day. He must have come here afterwards. *He* had a ladder, and a cigarette hanging out of his mouth!'

Emily sighed. Of course, Jack was right. 'We should still double-check,' she said defiantly. 'It's vital to be thorough in any investigation!'

Emily dispatched the boys to find Russ Kerrow – the only window-cleaner in Castle Key – to photograph his footprints and check which brand of cigarette he smoked, and to carry out house-to-house enquiries along Church Lane. Meanwhile, she planned to interview Adam Martin, the older brother of one of her friends at school. Adam and his gang went in for graffiti and other minor crimes such as crowning the statue of The Brave Cornish Fishermen on the seafront with traffic cones. Maybe they'd branched out into a spot of light house-breaking to liven up the long summer holiday.

Emily found Adam and his mates hanging around the

skateboard half-pipe in the park. But when she suggested the boys could have broken into Lilac Cottage, Adam shook his head so hard his nose-rings jingled.

'No way! Mrs Roberts used to let us draw cartoons in class. She said I had a gift for art!' His three mates laughed and one of them pulled a can of orange paint out of the pocket of his baggy jeans and pretended to spray it at Adam. But they all agreed. Mrs Roberts was *alright!*

When the team reported back at the tree house HQ later that afternoon, progress on Operation Break-in was precisely zero. The footprint and cigarette end *did* belong to Russ Kerrow, and none of the neighbours on Church Lane had heard or seen anything suspicious on the night of the burglary.

'That's it!' Emily cried. At last she'd remembered what it was that had been bothering her about the break-in. 'None of the neighbours heard anything!'

Jack shrugged. 'Yeah, that's what we just said.'

'But *why* didn't they hear anything?' Emily asked.

Jack had a feeling this was almost certainly a trick question. He kept quiet.

'Er, because they were asleep?' Scott suggested. 'Or because the burglars didn't make much noise?'

'But how did they get anywhere near Lilac Cottage without Biscuit barking his head off?' Emily asked. 'He wouldn't let an *earwig* cross that garden without barking at it, let alone someone jimmying open a window and climbing in through the conservatory! And Biscuit's pretty loud. I'm sure someone would have heard that racket in the middle of the night. Which means . . .'

'. . . the burglar has to be someone well-known to Mrs Roberts!' Scott finished the sentence. 'Someone Biscuit wouldn't bark at. Of course! That's brilliant!' He reached over to Emily for a high-five.

'Well, that narrows it down a bit,' Jack said. 'Mrs Roberts doesn't strike me as a party animal.'

'I've never seen anyone go to Lilac Cottage apart from her daughter, Laura,' Scott agreed. 'Oh, and Aunt Kate pops round for a coffee now and then.'

Emily looked up with a doubtful smile. 'So that's our suspect list? Laura Roberts and Aunt Kate. It doesn't give us much to work with, does it?'

—

When Emily got home to The Lighthouse she found her mum sitting on one of the sofas in the big circular guest lounge on the ground floor, chatting in Spanish to a new guest staying at their Bed and Breakfast. In a pink silk blouse, tailored shorts and diamante-studded sandals, the lady was so elegant she looked as if she'd stepped out of a magazine advert for something small and expensive – like watches or diamond earrings. She definitely didn't look as if she'd come for the bird-watching, hiking or surfing – which were the major tourist attractions on offer in Castle Key.

'This is Bianca Mendez,' Mum said, still speaking Spanish. 'She's from Chile. She's staying a few days while she researches an article on traditional Cornish fishing villages. Isn't that exciting?'

Although she was originally from Madrid, Mum didn't speak Spanish often – except when she lost her temper – but she was clearly enjoying the chance of a natter with a fellow Spanish speaker.

Bianca Mendez smiled at Emily. At least her mouth smiled. The rest of her face, including the dark eyes with their black eyeliner, didn't bother to join in. She held out her hand. Her nails were varnished in a pale pink and were so long they curled over at the end. Emily knew that she could be the tiniest smidgeon over-suspicious now and then, but *honestly*! Was she *really* meant to believe this lady was a serious journalist? There was no way she could type much more than an email address with talons like that!

'Which magazine do you write for?' Emily asked innocently.

Bianca patted her glossy black hair. 'Oh, it's a luxury lifestyle and international travel publication. *You* wouldn't know it.' She held Emily's gaze with a look in her eye as glittering – and as hard – as diamonds. Soon after that she got up to leave for her room.

'Will you be here for lunch tomorrow, Bianca?' Mum called after her.

Bianca took a few more steps, then suddenly realized she was being spoken to. She turned and smiled. 'No, I think I'll be eating out, thank you, Maria.'

As Emily climbed the one hundred and twenty steps of the spiral staircase to her room, she wondered about Bianca Mendez. She wondered a lot. And it wasn't just the fingernails. It was those few extra steps too. *Bianca didn't turn back as soon as Mum called her name.*

Of course, there was always the possibility she had a hearing impairment.

Or, *maybe* it took her a moment to remember she was going under the name Bianca? Oh, yes, Emily was quite sure Bianca was not who she seemed. *I'd better keep her under surveillance for a day or two,* she thought.

＊

So, when Bianca Mendez set off after breakfast next morning to 'wander around and soak up the atmosphere', Emily and Drift were not far behind.

They followed at a safe distance as Bianca picked her way along the narrow path from The Lighthouse into the village, and up and down the narrow lanes and alleys that ran between the high street and the seafront. The weather was still as sultry as a tropical rainforest. The storm had not yet broken and the clouds were gathering, ever darker, over the bay.

Bianca kept stopping and staring at people. She

peered into shops and even the windows of houses. Was this all part of the *soaking* process, Emily wondered. But then, why did Bianca keep looking back at a photo in her hand? It was almost as if she was searching for someone. But who could a glamorous lady from Chile want to find in Castle Key?

Bianca stopped to contemplate a group of fishermen unloading their catches in the harbour, then started walking back along the seafront. Suddenly, a rogue breeze whisked in from the bay and snatched the photo out of her manicured hand. The photo fluttered over the harbour wall and skipped across the beach towards the waves. Bianca opened her mouth and took a step forward.

Emily seized her chance. She gave the command. 'Drift, *Fetch*!'

Drift sailed over the wall and sprinted along the beach, delighted to stretch his legs after a morning of Stalking Duty, trudging round Castle Key after that lady at the pace of a geriatric poodle. He caught the paper between his teeth and bounded back. Emily took it from his jaws and waved to Bianca.

'Excuse me!' she called. 'I think you've dropped something!'

She handed the photograph over.

Not before sneaking a peek at it, of course.

'Thank you!' Bianca almost broke a nail in her haste to snatch the photo out of Emily's hand.

'Good work, Drift,' Emily murmured, burying her head in his fur to hide the look of astonishment on her face.

The photograph was a screenshot from the Cake Tent video.

It showed a pretty blonde girl trying to lasso a charging donkey with a halter.

It seemed Bianca Mendez was looking for Laura Roberts!

Five

Emergency Call-out

'Laura Roberts?' Scott echoed.

'That's right!' Emily's voice over the mobile phone was urgent.

'Let me get this straight,' Scott said slowly. 'An International Woman of Mystery from Chile turns up at The Lighthouse. You're following her because she's got long fingernails and she took three steps before telling your mum she'd be out to lunch? And she's searching for Laura Roberts?'

'Correct!' Emily said. 'And it won't be long before someone points her to the riding stables. So, get on your bikes and meet me there. We've got to find out what she's up to!'

Jack looked up from the hammock he was installing above the platform of the tree house. He'd found it rolled up in the corner of the shed and asked Aunt Kate if he could hang it between two tree branches in the garden. He hadn't exactly mentioned that the branches he had in mind were ten metres above the ground, but then she hadn't asked!

'What's that about chillies?' Jack asked. 'That reminds me, I've not had a good curry in weeks!'

'*Chile,* not chillies!' Scott said. 'As in the South American country. I'll explain on the way.'

Reluctantly Jack left the hammock and scrambled down the swaying rope ladder. 'We need a fireman's pole if we're going to be doing emergency call-outs!' he grumbled.

—

Roshendra Farm was about a mile from Castle Key, at the end of a narrow track that wound its way inland across the moors. The boys cycled as fast they could in the overpowering heat, hardly noticing the sheep and ponies grazing among the white tufts of cotton grass, or the buzzards soaring overhead.

The riding stables were set apart from the main farmhouse. A cluster of low stone buildings bordered a small yard. Beyond that was an outdoor riding arena and a series of paddocks dotted with cones and jumps. Several cars were parked on the cracked concrete near the entrance. Two teenage girls were mucking out a stable, watched by the soft dark eyes of a jet-black pony poking his head over the door of the next stall.

Scott and Jack spotted Emily's bike leaning against the trunk of an old oak tree. They parked their bikes next to it, crept round the back of the stable block and found Emily and Drift, peeping around the end of the building.

Laura Roberts was standing in the middle of the arena, calling out instructions to three little girls on ponies. 'And trot to A, and walk . . .' She was wearing riding boots, mud-stained jodhpurs, and an old blue t-shirt advertising Roshendra Riding Stables. She was about seventeen or eighteen, although her blonde plaits, wide blue eyes and pretty, turned-up nose sprinkled with freckles made her look younger.

Four ladies were sitting on a bench at the edge of the arena. Three of them were chatting and watching the lesson; they were clearly the mothers of the mini horse-riders. The fourth sat apart, looking as out of place as a parrot in a flock of seagulls: deeply tanned, hair like black treacle, designer sunglasses, sparkly sandals, and of course, those long pink fingernails.

'That's Bianca Mendez,' Emily said. She shook her head sadly. 'Laura must have got herself mixed up with some kind of international drug-smuggling ring.' Then she had an idea. 'Of course! That could be why Laura broke into her mum's house and stole the pictures and the money. She needs to pay off some debts to the ringleader or something!'

'International drug-smuggling?' Jack snorted. 'I can't see Laura as a *county*-level smuggler, let alone *international*!' In fact, Laura Roberts looked like the kind of girl whose darkest secret involved scoffing a tub of ice cream while watching a Twilight Saga movie. And, anyway, if she needed serious money, there'd be better places to look for it than Lilac Cottage.

'Shhh!' Scott hissed.

The lesson was over. Laura was helping the girls down from the ponies and talking with the mums. After they'd left, she looped the ponies' reins over the fence-posts and began loosening their girths. 'Come on, Piper! No, I haven't got any treats in my pocket!' she laughed as a plump little piebald nuzzled her side.

Bianca Mendez rose to her feet and picked her way across the dusty arena. 'Hello, you must be Laura?'

Laura looked up and smiled. 'Can I help you?'

'I was at school with your mother.' Bianca Mendez patted Piper's mane. 'We were such good friends but we lost touch. I'm trying to track her down. You look *so* like her!'

Laura moved onto the next pony and ran up the stirrups. 'Hey, that's brilliant. Mum'll be so excited. I thought she'd lost touch with all her old friends. Hang on, I'll give her a call.'

'Oh, no,' Bianca said quickly. 'Don't do that. I want it to be a surprise. Just tell me where she lives.'

Jack, Scott and Emily looked at each other. It wasn't *Laura* Roberts Bianca was hunting for, after all. It was *Mrs Roberts.*

'I guess that means we're cycling back to Lilac Cottage!' Jack said.

—

When they puffed and panted their way into Church Lane, Bianca Mendez's hire car was already parked outside Lilac Cottage. Raised voices were blaring out through the living-room window, accompanied by Biscuit's usual high-voltage barking.

'Sounds like World War Three going on in there!' Jack commented as they ducked down behind the garden fence to listen in.

'We *must* do the Trago House!' Bianca was yelling.

'What's the Trago House?' Scott whispered.

'It's an art gallery,' Emily said. 'That funny old building you can see up on the headland at the other end of the bay from the castle. It's where Digory Trago lived.'

Scott and Jack exchanged blank looks.

'Are we meant to know who that is?' Jack asked.

Emily grinned. 'You're obviously not experts on modern art, darlings! Trago's a mega-famous Cornish artist. Well, he was until he died last year. Now his house has been turned into an art gallery.'

'It has to be soon!' Bianca was insisting. 'I can't hang about!'

Wow, that Bianca must be dead keen on art, Jack thought. She was really throwing her toys out of the pram about going to the gallery. He could understand if it was the X Games finals or a Formula One Grand Prix or something, but an *art gallery*? What was the big deal with standing around staring at old paintings? And why couldn't she just go on her own, anyway? What a drama queen!

'No, I can't and I won't!' Mrs Roberts was shouting now. 'I've left all that behind!'

'Oh, you think so, do you?' Bianca sounded furious. 'Well, if you don't help me, I'll . . .'

Jack didn't find out what Bianca would do if her old friend didn't take her to the art gallery because Mrs Roberts must have suddenly realized that her monster row was being broadcast to half of Castle Key, and she slammed the window closed.

Jack felt a bit sorry for Mrs Roberts. First her house was burgled, then the Old School Friend from Hell turned up on her doorstep. She wasn't having a good week. And it was only Tuesday.

A moment later the front door flew open. The three friends dived for cover among the lilac bushes as Bianca Mendez marched down the path, almost pulled the garden gate off its hinges and threw herself into her car. She gunned the engine and, with a screech of tyres, reversed down Church Lane faster than Jenson Button on a final lap.

Scott raked his hands through his floppy brown hair. 'Whoa! If Bianca is Mrs Roberts' *friend*, I hope her *enemies* don't turn up.'

But Emily was already ringing the doorbell. Biscuit – who had only just finished his bark-fest over Bianca's departure – now started up again. Scott and Jack hurried to join Emily as Mrs Roberts opened the door a crack and peeped out.

'It's only us,' Emily said. 'We heard a disturbance. We were worried the burglars might have come back.'

Mrs Roberts sniffed. Her eyes were red and watery behind her glasses. 'Oh, no, everything's fine.' She managed a smile. 'It was just . . . an old friend of mine visiting.'

'We thought we heard an argument,' Scott ventured.

Mrs Roberts' face stiffened. 'Not really. It was just a little disagreement. Oh, look, here comes Laura,' she said, clearly relieved to change the subject.

Laura was hurrying up the path, bringing the sweet, earthy smell of horse manure and hay with her. She said hello to Scott, Jack and Emily and stroked Drift and Biscuit. Then she kissed her mother.

'I've popped over between lessons. I'm *dying* to know how you got on with that old friend of yours. She's a bit of a Glam Queen, isn't she? Like something out of *Vogue*!'

Mrs Roberts wiped her nose with a shredded tissue. 'Yes, she always was a snappy dresser.'

Laura held out a large, flat package. 'I went into Carrickstowe on the bus this morning and got this for you from the art shop. It's a replacement for your *Lady in Blue*. I know that one was your favourite. It's printed on canvas so it looks authentic and old and everything. And it's in a really nice frame. Come on, let's go and hang it up!'

As they said goodbye, Emily's thoughts were buzzing. Was it just a coincidence that Bianca had turned up the day after Mrs Roberts' house was burgled? Or were the two events connected somehow? Emily knew she'd been right all along: there was definitely more to the break-in than met the eye. And there was another thing she felt sure of: Bianca Mendez was *not* an old school-friend of Mrs Roberts any more than she was a journalist for a South American travel magazine! How many more layers would they have to peel away before they found the truth? *Perhaps,* Emily thought, *we should rename this investigation Operation Onion, after all!*

Six

Adventure in the Storm

That evening Emily was sitting on her bed writing up
the day's progress on Operation Break-in-Slash-
Onion. She kept replaying the snippets of conversation
they'd overheard between Mrs Roberts and Bianca.
Why was Bianca so keen to go to the Trago Gallery?
And – just as puzzling – why didn't Mrs Roberts want
to take her? Mrs Roberts worked at the gallery as a
volunteer guide a couple of days a week so you'd think

she'd *love* the chance to show her old friend around.

Emily took her binoculars and gazed out of the window across the bay. She had a three-hundred-and-sixty-degree view from her room at the top of The Lighthouse. The Trago Gallery perched on the headland at the western end of the bay. The dark shape of the building – as twisted and higgledy-piggledy as a Disneyland haunted house – was backlit by the sunset, which gilded the edges of the black storm clouds with Calpol pink and Lucozade orange. It was still unbearably hot. Emily was sure she wouldn't be able to sleep. She wished the storm would hurry up and break.

Suddenly she caught sight of a movement on the promontory directly below her. A black-clad figure was hurrying away from The Lighthouse towards the village. Emily opened her bedroom door and stood listening at the top of the spiral staircase. Mum and Dad were watching TV in the family living room several floors below. There were only three guests staying at The Lighthouse at the moment. The Scottish honeymoon couple had driven off to see a show in Truro earlier. That only left one person who could be sneaking off into the night: *Bianca Mendez*!

'Come on, Drift, we're on duty!' Emily pulled a dark fleece and tracksuit bottoms over her pyjamas and slung her bag over her shoulder. With Drift in her arms to stop the tell-tale clicking of his claws on the stairs, she tiptoed down to the front door, holding her breath as she passed the living room. It wasn't that Mum and Dad would mind her popping outside in the evening. They weren't strict about bedtimes in the summer holidays – and Drift had to do his business, after all – but Emily knew she'd risk losing track of Bianca if her parents waylaid her on the stairs for a chat. On the way past the kitchen she scribbled *Back in five minutes* on the chalkboard they used for messages. Then she crossed out *five* and wrote *ten*. She wanted plenty of time to see what Bianca was up to.

—

Emily and Drift knew every twist and turn of the path along the promontory and were soon catching up with Bianca, who had to tread carefully to avoid taking an unplanned dive into the waves below. When they came to the point where the promontory joined the harbour, Emily ducked down behind a rock. She expected Bianca to make for her hire car – parked in one of the spaces reserved for guests at The Lighthouse. That would mean giving up the chase, of course. But to her surprise, Bianca slipped past the cars and padded along the seafront – she'd changed her sparkly sandals for black trainers – sticking to the shadows, as stealthy as a panther.

Emily and Drift crept along behind her. They reached the far end of the harbour and passed the hulking metal ice works. The machines were humming away producing ice for the fishing boats and clouds of steam puffed out from the vents as if a giant dragon were trapped inside. It was dark now, apart from a glimmer of moonlight breaking through a gap in the storm clouds, but the air was still thick and humid. Emily was sweltering inside her tracksuit and fleece. Drift's tongue lolled from his mouth. Emily knew she'd been out far longer than the ten minutes she'd written on her note. She kept telling herself she'd only go a few more steps, but somehow she couldn't bear to turn back now. She *had* to know what Bianca was doing.

Bianca hurried on, joining the coast road that zigzagged its way up over the headland, lighting her way with a torch. She stopped on a hairpin bend in the road and played the torch beam over the steep rocky slope that stretched up to the crest of the headland, where the Trago Gallery loomed: a crazy jumble of towers, domes, walkways and arches. Then she left the road and struck out across the rocks, scrambling up towards the gallery. Emily had to admit, Bianca was a swift and skilful climber. In the moonlight she could make out the shadowy figure crouched on the rock, taking equipment from her backpack. *What was she doing?* Then Emily heard a scraping and hammering sound. *Was Bianca collecting rock samples?*

Suddenly Emily felt a cold splash on her nose. And another. Raindrops the size of water balloons were plunking onto the ground. The storm had finally broken. A flash of lightning ripped the sky open. Emily saw Bianca Mendez silhouetted against the electric white light, her black hair streaming with rainwater, a hammer in one hand, a torch in the other. Then darkness swallowed her up again. Thunder rumbled around the bay, echoing off the cliffs.

It was time to go. But as she and Drift backed away, Emily caught a loose rock with her foot. It tumbled down the cliff, dislodging more stones in a mini-avalanche. Emily knew instantly that she was in trouble. *Bianca must have heard that.* 'Freeze!' she hissed to Drift and ducked down among the thin scrubby bushes. Her heart flapped like a startled seagull. Drift's panting in her ear sounded as loud as a steam engine. *It's OK, she won't see us if we keep still,* Emily told herself. But when lightning flashed across the sky once more, she saw that Bianca was holding something up to her eyes. It was too dark for binoculars. *Bianca had night vision goggles.*

Emily held her breath. She was trapped on the headland. If she tried to go back down the road, Bianca would see her. But how long could she wait for Bianca to finish her mysterious excursion and leave? The rain was torrential now, the storm growing wilder by the minute. There was only one thing for it. Emily remembered a tiny rabbit path that ran down the headland below the road, and it came out somewhere along here. She just had to find it in the dark and the rain. She pushed the ribbons of dripping hair out of her eyes and whispered to Drift to follow. Then, crawling on her belly like a snake, Emily wriggled though the undergrowth, all the while praying that Bianca wouldn't catch sight of her. At last, they came to a spot where the long grass was trodden down. *This was it!* The footing was slick with rain, but Emily had been exploring these rocks for years and she was able to pick her way along the path. Drift ran along ahead to show the way. At the bottom of the headland the little track rejoined the road. Emily glanced behind to make sure Bianca wasn't following and raced along the harbour to the promontory.

Now all she had to do was to slip back into The Lighthouse without being noticed. But to her horror, she saw light shining from the open front door. Dad was staring out into the night. *Oh, no,* Emily thought. *They must have realized I'm missing. I've been over an hour. In a storm! Mum and Dad have probably had search parties out scouring the cliffs. They'll have called the police and the coastguard.* Fear and guilt welled up inside her – she hadn't meant to worry them. She'd only *meant* to be gone ten minutes. Her parents were more laid-back than most, but even *they* were going to freak out over this. She'd be grounded for weeks, locked in her bedroom at the top of The Lighthouse, like Rapunzel in her tower . . .

'Oh, there you are, Emski!' Dad called. 'Come on in out of that rain.'

Emily was so surprised she stopped in her tracks and tripped over Drift. She'd been psyching herself up to fall at Dad's feet, pleading for forgiveness. But Dad didn't even sound angry or upset. *What was going on?*

'I just saw your note on the board,' Dad said, pulling Emily inside and bundling her hair into a towel. 'I have to say, Drift picked a great moment to want to go out. And you're covered in mud!'

'Slipped over,' Emily mumbled, her fingers crossed behind her back. She'd always hated having her hair dried with a towel, especially by Dad, who rubbed so hard he practically decapitated her every time, but right now she had no objections. She was almost fainting with relief. 'Thanks, Dad!' she said, her voice muffled by the towel.

Emily turned to close the door and saw Bianca hurrying along the path towards them. She had a feeling it would be better if Bianca didn't see her. She grabbed the towel and made for the stairs. 'I'm really tired. Night, Dad.'

'G'night,' Dad said. He stood holding the door open for Bianca.

Emily hovered on the first-floor landing.

'Did you have a nice evening in Carrickstowe?' Dad asked.

'Yes, thank you, Seth,' Bianca replied. 'I went to a

movie.' Then she laughed. 'What a night! I'm soaked, just running back from the car.'

Emily resisted the urge to run downstairs shouting *Liar, liar, pants on fire!* Instead she went up to her room and set her alarm for an early start. She couldn't wait to tell the boys all about her late-night adventure in the storm!

Seven

Seriously Weird

N ext morning Emily popped up through the platform of the tree house bursting with the story.

The storm had passed, and the weather was clear and sunny once more. Jack was lounging in the hammock among the chestnut leaves, with the dappled sunlight warm on his face. He was so intrigued by Bianca's nocturnal rock-climbing expedition that he leaned over to hear better. Unfortunately he moved a little too fast. The hammock flipped him over and deposited him on the platform beneath. He nearly landed on top of Drift – who had just been hoisted up in his basket.

Jack sat up and brushed himself down. 'Just checking the, er, Ejector Mechanism and the Emergency Landing Procedures on the old hammock! All seem to be in order.' He stood up and fiddled with the ropes as if making a slight adjustment.

Emily laughed and continued her account. 'I think Bianca is planning to break into the Trago Gallery and make her getaway down the cliff. That's what she was doing last night – figuring out the best way down. She's *obviously* an international art thief!'

Scott was not convinced. 'Yeah, right! If she's planning a robbery, why did she do such a big number about wanting Mrs Roberts to show her around the gallery? Talk about making it obvious! She doesn't *look* like a total space cadet!'

Jack grinned. 'No, she looks like Cruella de Vil – that mad lady in *One Hundred and One Dalmatians* who goes round making puppies into fur coats. Sorry, Drift!' he added, clapping his hands over the little dog's velvety ears. 'Didn't mean to upset you there!'

Emily laughed again, then returned to Scott's point. 'I can't work out why Bianca went to see Mrs Roberts either. It wasn't exactly your typical reunion, was it? At first I thought Bianca was trying to con money out of her somehow. You know, like Simon Fox . . .'

Jack knew what she meant. As well as stealing the friends' treasure map, Simon 'Psycho' Fox had been tricking elderly people into investing in his dodgy deals. But that was their *last* mystery! Surely Cruella wasn't up to the same old scam?

'But if she's an *art thief*,' Emily continued, 'she's probably trying to trick Mrs Roberts into telling her the security codes at the gallery or something!'

Jack grinned. Emily was like a mind-reader when it came to crime. If she ever crossed over to the dark side, she'd be an evil genius! He climbed back into the hammock, parted the leaves and gazed down at Lilac Cottage. Biscuit was zipping about the neat little garden like a deflating balloon, barking at a squirrel. How did someone as *ordinary* as Mrs Roberts get to be school-friends with someone like Cruella anyway? Then again, Jack thought, conjuring up a mental image of his class, there were probably a few criminal masterminds among his mates in the back row!

Emily made some notes in her book. 'We need to talk to Mrs Roberts and see if she has any idea what Bianca is up to.'

Scott agreed. He still didn't believe that Bianca was really an art thief, but she was definitely a bit mysterious. There'd be no harm in asking Mrs Roberts a few questions about her.

Emily glanced at her watch. 'It's 10.37 a.m. Mrs Roberts

will be at the Trago Gallery now. She always works there Wednesday mornings. We can talk to her there.'

Scott was always amazed at how Emily knew the precise movements of every inhabitant of Castle Key. 'What time does she have her tea break?' he teased.

Emily thought for a moment. 'Half past eleven,' she replied. 'Except for the last Friday of the month, when they have a staff meeting. What are you laughing at?'

'Oh, nothing!' Scott said quickly.

'Do we have to go *now*?' Jack groaned. 'I've just got comfortable again.'

Scott couldn't resist grabbing the hammock and tipping Jack out onto the platform again. 'Just double-checking that Ejector Mechanism,' he laughed, legging it down the ladder before Jack could catch him. 'Yep, it seems pretty reliable!'

The Trago Gallery was the strangest building Scott had ever seen. It looked as if a mad scientist had been experimenting with gingerbread houses and the leftover pieces had mutated in his laboratory overnight.

'Digory Trago built it himself,' Emily said. 'He lived here for over fifty years and kept adding bits on to it right up until he died. He was a bit eccentric!'

'*Eccentric*?' Scott laughed. 'That'd be the polite word for barking mad, then?'

Emily watched as Scott and Jack tried to open the front door at the top of the stone steps. 'This isn't budging!' Jack shouted.

Emily laughed. 'False door!'

Scott looked closer. What *looked* like a heavy wooden door was actually painted straight onto the wall. The real door was much smaller, and set off to one side!

The inside of the house was so random it made the outside look positively sensible! The floor of the vast entrance hall was tiled in black and white squares, and a series of marble columns disappeared into the distance. Except, Scott soon realized, they were only painted to look like marble, and the distance was a trick of perspective. The hall was really only a normal size – as he found out when he walked into a wall of mirrors! It was all seriously weird – but in a seriously cool way!

'The main gallery's this way,' Emily said, heading towards a staircase, past furniture with human-shaped arms and legs, a fountain with purple water that seemed to run uphill, and a menagerie of enormous stuffed animals. There was even a flying pig hanging from the ceiling, complete with angel wings and a little tiara.

'This place is *totally* awesome!' Jack said, sticking his tongue out at himself in a distorting mirror. 'Why didn't you tell us about it before?'

'I did,' Emily said. 'Weeks ago.'

'Yeah, but you said *art gallery*. That means dusty old portraits and pictures of flowers and stuff. I didn't know it was . . .' Jack gestured at his surroundings, momentarily lost for words, '. . . *insane!*'

The stairs didn't exactly move around Hogwarts-style, but they were just as bizarre. Some flights stopped in mid-air, while others looked as if they went down but actually went up. But eventually the friends came to the main gallery. The huge paintings were all skewed drunkenly at different angles. Trago's paintings featured grotesque figures running around impossible buildings, tropical flowers made up of thousands of tiny insects, eggs that looked like eyeballs. *This Trago guy had some* serious *issues*, Scott thought.

'There she is!' Emily pointed to the end of the gallery.

'What's she *doing*?' Jack asked as they drew closer.

Mrs Roberts was staring at a painting of an orchestra. Or at least, Digory Trago's version of an orchestra; the musicians were all wild animals and their instruments were actually growing out of their bodies. Mrs Roberts was busy inspecting an elephant with a tuba for a trunk. Then she took a magnifying glass from her handbag and peered through it at a mutant being, half zebra, half piano.

'Looks like she's really into that painting,' Scott said.

'No accounting for taste!' Emily giggled. 'It's horrible!'

'Don't look, Drifty,' Jack said, covering the little dog's eyes. 'It'll give you nightmares!'

Now Mrs Roberts was looking at her mobile phone.

She glanced around and noticed she was being watched. She hastily stuffed the phone back in her bag and smiled nervously.

'Er, nice painting,' Jack said. 'Very interesting, er, interpretation of the er . . .' he struggled to sound as if he knew what he was talking about.

Mrs Roberts smiled again. 'Digory Trago was a master of the *surreal* style of painting. This is one of his finest works.'

'Bet it's worth a packet then?' Jack asked.

Mrs Roberts gulped and fiddled with the buttons on her cardigan. 'Well, er, yes, Trago's work has become very valuable in the art market since his death.'

'It must have been a nice surprise to see your friend, Bianca, again?' Scott asked politely.

Mrs Roberts' brow furrowed. 'Oh, yes, very nice!' she said, vaguely.

'Have you seen much of her since you left school?' Scott pressed.

Mrs Roberts shook her head. 'Oh, no, I've not seen Nina for years.'

'Nina?' Emily asked.

Mrs Roberts wiped her hands down the front of her plain beige dress as if her palms were sweating. 'Oh, Nina was, er, Bianca's sister. I was always getting them muddled.'

There was a clackety-clack of heels across the tiles. They all looked up to see Bianca Mendez striding towards them in a low-cut white linen dress, sunglasses pushed up onto her raven hair.

'Ah, there you are . . . *Jean*! So kind of you to show me around this morning.' She glanced at the animal orchestra and aimed a lipsticked smile at Mrs Roberts. She ignored Emily, Scott, Jack and Drift – as if they were just one of the gallery's optical illusions. 'I do *love* Trago's work!'

'Oh yes . . . er . . .' Mrs Roberts had looked anxious before, but now the last dregs of colour drained from her face, as if she'd seen a ghost, rather than a long-lost friend.

As Emily smiled and said goodbye, her thoughts were as mixed up as one of Trago's paintings.

The Trago Gallery was certainly weird. But Mrs Roberts' behaviour was weirder still!

Eight

Skeletons in the Cupboard

The three friends free-wheeled down the winding road back into Castle Key. Jack and Scott were racing as if they were in the giant slalom in the Winter Olympics. Jack was in the lead, his bike banking over so far on the bends, his knees almost scraped along the ground. Emily caught them up and found Jack laughing at Scott's long sun-streaked hair. The wind had swept it off his face and the salty sea air – as strong as extra-hold hair gel – had sculpted it into a quiff like a giant Mr Whippy ice cream. Scott began frantically patting it back down. 'What next?' he asked.

'I vote we go to Dotty's for lunch,' Jack said. 'Studying surrealist art *always* gives me an appetite.'

Scott snorted. 'Yeah, right! You've never even *seen* any surrealist art before!'

Jack grinned. 'Precisely. Now I have. And I'm hungry. I rest my case!'

A few moments later the friends had parked their bikes and were sitting down to lunch at an outside table on the seafront.

Jack fed a chip to Drift under the table. When he looked up he saw a figure in an orange high-visibility vest and a helmet, aiming a pressure hose at the wall of the Castle Key Cabin nearby. At first he thought it was a fireman tackling a fire, but then he saw that the helmet was a pink bicycle helmet with a Cinderella figure on the front, and it was perched on top of tight grey curls. Mrs Loveday! The hunched figure was cleaning graffiti off the wall, clinging on with all her strength to stop the hose writhing out of control and catapulting her over the harbour wall into the bay like a human cannonball.

Jack looked at the giant blue, orange and white letters beneath the jet of water and did a double take. They spelled the word *AM-EN*. Had the *vicar* been out tagging the walls along the seafront? Or maybe it was Colin Warnock, the curate, with his posse of radical bell-ringers?

Emily laughed. 'No, it's Adam Martin and his gang. A and M are his initials, of course, and E N stands for Extreme Network. Adam's sister told me.'

'Extreme Network? What does that mean?' Jack asked.

Emily shrugged. 'No idea! They probably just think it sounds cool.'

The friends watched as Mrs Loveday wrestled the pressure hose to the ground as if it was a giant anaconda. She switched it off and opted for a more traditional scrubbing brush approach.

'So,' Scott said, biting into his Cornish pasty, 'what's the deal with Mrs Roberts? She was looking at that animal orchestra painting as if it contained the meaning of life!'

'And why is she so scared of Bianca?' Emily asked. 'There must be some history there. I'm starting to think Bianca could be a spy. A double agent, possibly. Maybe Mrs Roberts is her contact.'

Jack nearly dropped his fork. 'Shh! Mrs Loveday will hear you,' he whispered. 'You know what a nosy parker she is!'

Scott thought for a moment. 'Hang on. Maybe we *want* Mrs Loveday to hear us.'

Jack stared at him as if he'd just suggested that they might *want* to go ballet-dancing naked down the high street.

'What do you mean?' Emily asked.

Scott looked over his shoulder. Mrs Loveday had popped inside to fetch another bucket of water. 'If Mrs Roberts has any secrets – you know, any skeletons in the cupboard – Mrs Loveday will know all about them.'

Jack snorted. 'Mrs Loveday won't just *know* about the skeletons. She'll have been in the cupboard polishing the bones!'

Scott laughed. 'Exactly! And if we just ask Mrs Loveday straight out about Mrs Roberts, that will make her suspicious. But if she overhears us *talking,* you know what she's like . . .'

Emily grinned. 'She'll be over here before you can say AM-EN! Scott, you're a genius!'

'I'm not one for tittle-tattle, but . . .' Scott said, imitating Mrs Loveday's favourite opening line.

Emily hushed him. 'Here she comes now.'

Jack's heart sank. He couldn't believe they were actually going to *encourage* Mrs Loveday to eavesdrop. It was like encouraging the seagulls to scavenge round your table by putting out bowls of bird-food! It was *unnatural.*

'Yeah, poor Mrs Roberts,' Emily said loudly, as if they

were in the middle of a conversation. 'That burglary must have been a nasty shock.'

'At least she's got a visitor to cheer her up a bit. She's staying at The Lighthouse, isn't she?' Scott asked.

'That's right. Bianca Mendez. An old school friend.'

Jack sighed. Surely Mrs Loveday wasn't going to fall for this. Emily and Scott sounded as if they were reading out lines from a play in a particularly dull English lesson! But he'd clearly underestimated Mrs Loveday's Gossip Detector. He could almost *see* her ears twitching – the way Drift's did when he heard a crisp packet being opened. And now she was sidling towards their table, pretending to scrub the café's windowsills.

Scott looked at his watch and grinned. 'Fifteen seconds,' he mouthed. 'Must be a world record!'

'Yobs!' Mrs Loveday announced, one hand on her hip and the other brandishing the scrubbing brush in the direction of the graffiti. 'Going around *togging* everything in sight.'

Jack tried to ignore the laughter bubbling up in his chest like hiccups. 'You mean *tagging*?'

'Well *you* obviously know rather a lot about the subject!' Mrs Loveday glared at Jack as if she'd caught him red-handed – or rather orange-blue-and-white-handed – holding the spray can. For some reason, Mrs Loveday had always regarded Jack as Public Enemy Number One. The feeling was mutual!

'That looks like hard work!' Scott said in his most understanding voice. 'Would you like a sit-down?'

Mrs Loveday beamed at him as if he'd offered her a three-week Caribbean cruise. 'Ooh, if only these Juvenile Detergents with their spray cans were more like you, dear!'

'Juvenile *delinquents*?' Scott corrected.

'They certainly are!' Mrs Loveday said.

Scott smiled, even though he thought the graffiti looked pretty cool. Not when it was daubed all over the seafront, perhaps, but the artwork was really original and skilfully done. 'Jack'll get you a cup of tea,' he said, kicking his brother under the table.

Jack muttered under his breath as he stomped inside to the counter. OK, he knew Scott was just buttering Mrs Loveday up to get her to talk but, even so, if he wanted to act like a prize creep, why couldn't he fetch his own stupid cups of stupid tea?

Mrs Loveday pulled up a chair. 'I couldn't help hearing you talking about Jean Roberts. Now, you know me, I'm not one for tittle-tattle, but . . .'

Scott and Emily held their breath, waiting for Mrs Loveday to reveal the truth about Mrs Roberts' double life as an arms dealer or secret agent.

Mrs Loveday took the cup of tea from Jack and thanked Scott. She looked as if she was about to speak, but then she frowned and shook her head. 'Actually, nobody has a bad word to say about her.'

Emily stared in disbelief. This had to be a first! Mrs Loveday had failed to come up with a single morsel of scandal. Not even an overdue library book or a parking ticket!

Mrs Loveday slurped her tea. 'Now where was I? Oh, yes, Jean Roberts. Her husband, Harry, ran the newsagents. He died of a heart attack a few years back. Jean taught art at the school until she retired last year. They only had the one daughter, Laura, she's a lovely girl too.'

'Has Mrs Roberts always lived in Castle Key?' Scott asked.

'Oh, no! She came about twenty-five years ago. Jean Chandler she was then. Married Harry a couple of years later.' Mrs Loveday paused for another gulp of tea. Her beady eyes flickered. 'Nobody knows anything about her life before she came to the island. She once told me all her old photos had been destroyed in a house fire. For all we know, she could have had a Misspelled Youth!'

'*Misspent* youth, you mean?' Emily asked.

'That's right, dear. She could have been out *togging* every night, like this lot!' Mrs Loveday pointed her teacup at the graffiti. 'Or worse! She could have been a shoplifter or a joyrider or one of those Glue Snufflers!'

'It's glue *sniffers*,' Jack said, trying not to laugh.

Mrs Loveday ignored him. By now she'd convinced herself that Mrs Roberts was a One-Woman Crimewave.

'Shocking! All those dark secrets lurking beneath the surface. Makes you think, doesn't it?'

Emily nodded politely. She couldn't see Mrs Roberts as a joyrider or a glue sniffer, somehow. But she did agree with Mrs Loveday on one thing: she was sure there was at least one dark secret in Jean Roberts' past.

A secret called Bianca Mendez.

Nine

The Copycat Gang

Emily groaned as a text popped up on her phone. 'Mum wants me on Cleaning Duty all afternoon.' She made a face at Scott and Jack. 'Don't suppose you'd like to come and help?' *Funny how the boys have suddenly remembered vitally important things they need to do this afternoon,* she thought. *Like cutting their toenails and arranging their music downloads into alphabetical order!* 'Looks like it's just you and me,

Drift,' she sighed, pushing her plate away and getting up from the café table. 'Hey, I wonder if Mrs Loveday would lend me that pressure hose? That'd speed things up a bit!'

—

Mum was wearing a paint-spattered kaftan and had her long hair tied up in something that looked suspiciously like a bright yellow duster. She was teetering on a stepladder in the guest lounge, swiping at the ceiling with a feather duster. At least there were no corners in the circular room for the spiders to hide in!

'Take all the cushions off the sofas, please,' Mum instructed. 'Clean behind them and then plump them up.'

Emily got to work, cleaning and plumping. There were four large sofas in the lounge. She was on the third, when she found the mobile phone. It must have fallen out of a pocket and slipped down between the cushions.

'Oh, that must be Bianca's!' Mum called down from the stepladder. 'She was sitting there this morning. She just went out. Put it on the reception desk. I'm sure she'll be back for it in a minute.'

Emily stared at the little phone in the palm of her hand. This could be her chance to find out Bianca's real name! She hurried past the reception desk and pretended to put the phone down.

'Just going to get some water for Drift,' she called.

Then she ran up to the kitchen, and with trembling fingers, clicked on *Settings* to see who the phone was registered to. *Bianca Mendez!* Emily's heart sank. Maybe she was wrong and that *was* her real name, after all? Or had Bianca been clever enough to register her phone under her false name? There must be another way to find out! But time was running out. Bianca could come back for her phone any moment. Desperately, Emily scrolled through the unfamiliar Spanish names in the contacts list. Suddenly, she saw an entry that leaped off the screen: *Mamá*! Surely Bianca's mother would know her real name! Emily called the number.

There was some beeping and whirring as the international connection went through. Then a woman's voice answered.

Emily realized she probably should have thought this through first. You couldn't just phone a number in Chile and pipe up with, 'You don't know me, but is your daughter using a false name?' She was going to have to make it up as she went along. 'Señora Garcia?' she asked, picking the first Spanish surname that came into her head.

The lady at the other end of the line sounded confused. '*No! Soy Señora* Rodriguez.'

'Oh, I'm so sorry,' Emily said politely in Spanish. 'I got mixed up. Is your daughter at home?'

'No. Nina doesn't live here any more.'

Nina? Emily did a Happy Dance with Drift round

the kitchen. She'd known it all along! When they were in the gallery Mrs Roberts had called Bianca 'Nina' by mistake! It was all falling into place. Bianca Mendez was *Nina Rodriguez!*

At that moment Emily heard the front door open downstairs

'*Gracias! Adiós!*' she mumbled into the phone. She rang off and flew down the spiral stairs. She reached the reception desk just as Bianca – or rather, Nina – entered the guest lounge. 'I think I must have dropped my . . .'

Emily looked up and smiled sweetly. '. . . your mobile phone?' She picked it up from the desk and held it out. 'I just found it down the back of the sofa.'

Emily had never worked so fast. She sped around the guest lounge like Mary Poppins on fast-forward while Drift hid under the desk in case she got carried away with the cleaning bug and had any wild ideas about giving him a bath. Two hours later every possible surface had been polished, vacuumed and dusted, and Mum said she could go. With a very relieved Drift at her heels, Emily sprinted to Stone Cottage.

The boys were kicking a ball around in the garden. Bonfire smoke was drifting over the hedge from the next-door garden, giving the late summer's afternoon an autumny smell. 'Oh, look. It's Cinders!' Jack laughed. 'She's been slaaaaaving away all afternoon.' He mimed a bit of tragic violin playing.

Emily caught the football. 'If I'm Cinderella, then you two must be the ugly sisters!'

Jack tried to knock the ball out of Emily's hands, but she dodged and held on to it. 'So, don't you want to hear about my breakthrough?'

'What breakthrough?' Scott panted, running after Emily. But she was as quick as a rabbit and dummied him with a sharp turn.

'Bianca's real name. It's Nina Rodriguez!' Emily ran for the flowerbed, dived and touched the ball down beneath a stand of hollyhocks. She had no idea how this had turned into a rugby match, but she'd just scored a try. Scott, Jack and Drift all piled on top of her.

Jack sat up and brushed leaves and petals from his shorts. 'Let me get this straight. Cruella de Vil isn't Bianca Mendez. She's Nina Rodriguez.'

Emily nodded.

'I hope you're keeping up with this, Drift,' Jack said, ruffling the little dog's fur and rolling over with him in a wrestling hold. Drift did his Happy Ears and joined the scrum. After Emily, Jack was Drift's favourite person in the world. He was more puppy than human!

'Come on!' Scott grabbed Emily's hand and pulled her out of the hollyhocks. 'Aunt Kate's busy making raspberry jam in the kitchen. We can use her computer.

Let's look up Nina Rodriguez and see what we can dig up on the internet.'

The sweet scent of molten jam enveloped them as they opened the door of Stone Cottage.

'Wow!' Jack gasped. 'This must be what heaven smells like!'

Scott sat down at the table in the living room and typed the name *Nina Rodriguez* into the search box. The computer was an antique and the connection was so slow you could do a bit of knitting while you waited for a file to open (Aunt Kate often did, Scott had noticed!). He stared at the screen, hardly able to wait for the results to pop up. Could Bianca/Nina really be an art thief, as Emily suspected? Scott had to admit, Bianca's false name and the night-time wanderings on the headland were decidedly dodgy. But maybe Bianca had just gone out for an evening stroll and lost her way on the rocks? If all Emily's suspicions turned out to be true, the entire population would be spies or smugglers or mass murderers. In Emily World, even *Aunt Kate* was probably an MI5 double agent . . .

'Here it is!' he shouted. Emily and Jack pulled up chairs and crowded round the screen. '*Nina Rodriguez: Copycat Gang,*' Scott read out. 'What's the Copyca—' but Jack had already grabbed the mouse and clicked on the link.

The webpage that came up on the screen was a blog about crime in the art world. Scott could hardly believe his eyes as he began to read:

During the 1980s the art world was rocked by a series of thefts carried out by the notorious Copycat Gang. The gang targeted leading galleries. They are thought to have stolen several Picassos from the Louvre in Paris, at least one Rembrandt from New York and Leonardo da Vinci's *Lady in Blue* from the National Gallery in London . . .

'*Lady in Blue*? Isn't that the one the burglars nicked from Lilac Cottage?' Jack asked.

'I imagine the original was *slightly* more valuable than an old print, though,' Scott laughed. 'Like a gazillion times more valuable!'

Aunt Kate came in from the kitchen with a plate of jam tarts warm from the oven. 'Oh, yes, the Copycat Gang,' she said, pausing behind Scott and peering over her glasses at the screen. 'I remember that gang well. It was the inspiration behind one of Dirk Hazard's best-known thrillers, *In the Frame.*'

Scott grinned. Dirk Hazard was Aunt Kate's favourite author. She had all his spy and crime novels on her shelves. If Aunt Kate ever went on *Mastermind*, he'd be her specialist subject. But right now she was under siege from an entire battalion of sugar-crazed wasps, zooming in on the smears of jam on her apron. She retreated to the kitchen to repel the attack.

Scott turned back to the screen and continued to read:

The Copycat Gang were so-called because they always replaced the stolen painting with a perfect forgery. In many cases, the theft went unnoticed for months or even years, by which time the original painting was untraceable. Gang leader, Juan Delgado, was brought to justice in 1992, but escaped from prison and has been living in South America ever since. The other known members of the gang were all women: Rosie McVey, Anita Nesbitt and Nina Rodriguez. They have never been caught.

'I was right!' Emily exclaimed, jumping up and hugging the computer screen. 'Bianca *is* an art thief! She's Nina Rodriguez of the Copycat Gang.'

'And she's going to strike again and steal a painting from the Trago Gallery,' Jack said, reaching up for a high-five.

'Yuk!' Emily groaned. 'Your hands are covered in jam!'

'And that's not the only thing,' Scott said. 'If *Bianca* was a member of the Copycat Gang, and she's an old friend of Mrs Roberts, *what if . . .*'

'. . . Mrs Roberts was in the Copycat Gang too!' Emily finished the sentence for him. 'That's *exactly* what I was thinking.'

Jack, Scott and Emily looked at each other wide-eyed with excitement. Now things were starting to get interesting. *Very* interesting indeed.

Ten

Hard Evidence

'*Nom, nom, nom!*' Jack mumbled, reaching for the plate again. These were seriously good jam tarts! And this was turning into a seriously good investigation. Never mind some boring old burglary at Mrs Roberts' house, with zero clues or suspects and hardly anything taken. This was more like it! A gang of art thieves. They even had a cool name, the Copycat Gang! Not to mention a mysterious leader, Juan Delgado, on the run in South America! And now, Nina Rodriguez had returned to steal a painting from the Trago Gallery. 'It's just like *Ocean's Eleven*!' he sighed happily.

'What are you on about?' Scott muttered.

'You know, that film with George Clooney. He gets a bunch of his old accomplices out of retirement to pull off a big casino heist. Cruella has come back to ask her old buddy, Mrs Roberts, to do this one last job with her!'

Emily nodded thoughtfully. 'Yes, I think you're right.'

Scott looked back at the article on the computer screen. 'So, if Mrs Roberts *was* in the gang, she must be one of these two: Rosie McVey or Anita Nesbitt.'

Jack laughed. 'It seems Mrs Loveday is right for once. Mrs Roberts *did* have a Misspelled Youth before she came to Castle Key. Only it was a bit classier than joyriding or pinching chocolate bars from the corner shop. She was nipping over to Paris, helping herself to masterpieces from the Louvre!' He had to admit, it was hard to imagine Aunt Kate's nice-but-frumpy next-door neighbour having a secret life as an international art thief. But then, *all* the best superheroes and villains had a day job as a mild-mannered Mr or Mrs Normal, didn't they? And it would explain why the inside of Lilac Cottage was so trendy and cool, while the outside looked so old-fashioned. Mrs Roberts was leading a fully-fledged double life! And there was something else, now he thought about it. 'Remember how Mrs Roberts was staring at that animal orchestra painting in the gallery? She had a magnifying glass and everything. I bet *that's* the painting they're planning to steal, and they're going to paint a copy of it to hang in its place.'

'Jack, you're a genius!' Emily leaped out of her chair and threw her arms around him. Then she leaped back, her brown skin flushing as pink as Aunt Kate's raspberry jam. 'Oops, sorry!' she said, as if she'd stood on his toe. 'That's it, of course! Mrs Roberts is a brilliant artist. She must have been the member of the Copycat Gang who painted the perfect forgeries. It all fits!'

Jack grinned. Even Scott was looking mildly impressed by this stroke of supreme awesomeness – although he was trying his best not to show it, of course.

Emily grabbed her bag and pulled out her notebook. 'We'll put Operation Break-in on hold.' She turned to a new page and wrote *OPERATION COPYCAT.*

Scott raked his fingers through his hair. 'I like Mrs Roberts but we're going to have to call the police and tip them off before she and Bianca steal the Trago painting.'

Emily shook her head. 'We need some hard evidence first.'

Jack jabbed at the screen, leaving a sticky fingerprint. 'What more do you want? *Hello!* They're the *Copycat Gang,* people!'

Emily sighed. 'All we have is *circumstantial* evidence. OK, we know Bianca Mendez is really Nina Rodriguez and that she was in the Copycat Gang. But we're only guessing that *Mrs Roberts* was one of the other two women in the gang. We need to be sure before we take this case to Detective Inspector Hassan.'

Scott nodded. 'Yeah, that's true. And we don't *know* that she's making a copy of Trago's animal orchestra painting. All we know for certain is that she was studying it closely. That's not exactly a crime! Especially not in an art gallery!' He leaned back in his chair. 'I should be able to find more information if I dig around on the internet – something to link Mrs Roberts to the Copycat Gang.'

Emily closed her notebook. 'While you do that, Jack and I will go round to Lilac Cottage and sneak a look in Mrs Roberts' studio. If our theory's right, we should find a half-finished copy of the animal orchestra on her easel!'

Shouting over the frantic barking, Mrs Roberts welcomed Emily, Jack and Drift into the living room at Lilac Cottage. Jack remembered hearing on a nature programme that the pistol shrimp snapping its claws together makes the loudest sound in the animal kingdom in relation to its body size. Whoever said that hadn't met Biscuit!

'I'm afraid we haven't had any more leads on your burglary,' Emily told Mrs Roberts. She glanced at the new print of the *Lady in Blue,* which was now hanging above the fireplace. The other pictures had not yet been replaced. The bare patches on the walls made the room feel somehow naked and fragile.

'We're wondering if the thief could be someone you know, because no one heard Biscuit barking,' Emily went on.

Mrs Roberts sank down onto the sofa. Her eyes were puffy, as if she'd been crying. Perhaps it was the smoke from the bonfire she'd had in her garden earlier, Emily thought. The smell of it still clung to her.

'Oh, well, never mind,' Mrs Roberts mumbled. She drummed nervously on her knees with her fingers. Her nails were chewed and ragged.

Emily felt sorry for her. If Mrs Roberts *had* gone back to her old life of crime she didn't seem to be enjoying it much. 'I hope all the worry hasn't affected your painting?' she said. 'What are you working on at the moment?'

'Yeah, can we have a look?' Jack butted in, cutting straight to the chase. He was halfway to the studio door already.

Emily glared at him. He sat back down with a shrug.

Mrs Roberts swallowed so hard she gave herself a coughing fit. 'Oh, no,' she spluttered. 'I don't like to show anyone my paintings before they're finished.'

Now Emily was more certain than ever that there was a copy of Trago's picture hidden in the studio. Last time they'd visited, Mrs Roberts had been more than happy to show them her work. All they needed was a minor distraction to get Mrs Roberts out of the room so they could sneak into the studio and snap a photo of the forgery in progress.

Suddenly Emily had an idea. *This could be the perfect moment to try out Drift's new command!* She bent down to give Drift a little cuddle – he was sitting at her feet watching Biscuit chew a rubber bone – and whispered one word in his ear: 'Distraction!'

Drift looked at her with his head on one side, his spotted ear pricked up to say *Are you sure about this?* This was a high-stakes command, to be used with extreme caution. Emily looked him in the eye and gave him a tiny nod. Drift panted happily. Distraction was, without doubt, the coolest command *ever* and he'd been dying to try it out for weeks. All he had to do was look for the naughtiest thing he could find to do and then – and this was the good part – *actually do it*! He barked to Biscuit to follow him and ran into the kitchen. Drift looked around for something *really* bad. If only there was a cat to chase! Then he spotted the plate of sausages defrosting on the table. *Oh, yes!* And if he played his cards right, he could even pass the blame off on Biscuit . . .

Mrs Roberts jumped out of her seat when she heard the crash in the kitchen. Her nerves were clearly on edge already; now they piled right *over* the edge like a flock of lemmings. 'Oh, my Lord!' she shouted. 'Whatever was that?' She ran into the kitchen. 'Oh! *Biscuit!* How *could* you?'

'Now!' Emily whispered, rocketing towards the studio door. Jack was right behind her. The first thing she saw was a collection of photos stuck on a pin-board, all showing details of the Trago painting: a violin with a lion's mane, a tiger-striped clarinet . . . So *that's* what Mrs Roberts was doing with her mobile phone in the gallery! She was taking pictures to help her with the forgery.

'This must be it!' Jack darted across to the big easel in the corner. An old grey blanket had been thrown over the top to hide the canvas beneath. 'Shall I do the honours?'

Emily pulled her phone out of her pocket and clicked it on to the camera function. She glanced over her shoulder. Mrs Roberts was still in the kitchen sweeping up the broken plate.

Emily gave a thumbs-up. 'Go for it!'

Eleven

The Moment of Truth

Meanwhile, Scott was so busy clicking his way through a trail of websites that his mouse finger was starting to seize up! But it seemed that Anita Nesbitt and Rosie McVey had both disappeared off the face of the planet.

Scott was about to give up and go and join the others when he hit the jackpot. An old newspaper article from 1984 described the theft of a priceless Picasso painting from a gallery in Rome. It included a small photograph of 'high-society girl, Samantha Burlington, believed by many to be the true identity of Anita Nesbitt, the brilliant forger at the heart of the Copycat Gang's success.'

No wonder I couldn't track down Anita Nesbitt, Scott thought. *That was a false name too.*

Scott zoomed in on the grainy photo. Samantha Burlington had been snapped getting out of a silver Rolls-Royce. She was wearing a blue dress with padded shoulders and a flouncy skirt. The *Lady in Blue*, Scott thought. Then he stared in disbelief. Fine blonde hair, upturned nose, wide blue eyes. He knew that face!

He made a spluttering noise, a mixture of shock and triumph, so loud that Aunt Kate hurried through from the kitchen to see whether he was choking on a jam tart.

The girl in the picture was Laura Roberts.

But it couldn't be, because *Laura Roberts wasn't even born in 1984*!

But of course! It wasn't *Laura* Roberts. It was *her mother*! But the plain dark-haired woman with her big glasses and baggy dresses was a million miles from the girl in the photograph. Mrs Roberts had given herself a total reverse-makeover. She must have had some plastic surgery too, to straighten her pretty upturned nose. Now Scott thought about it, it *had* seemed odd when Bianca told Laura Roberts at the riding stables that she looked just like her mother. She didn't look anything like her! But that's because Mrs Roberts didn't look anything like herself any more either!

Scott enlarged the photograph and pressed *print*. He tore the page from the printer and ran next door to show Emily and Scott.

He felt as if he'd scored a hat trick in a World Cup final. And, seeing that he was a defender, that would be pretty good going!

—

The front door of Lilac Cottage was ajar. Scott rang the bell but he knew Emily and Jack were there already so he walked straight in, through the hall and into the living room. To his surprise, it was empty. Sounds of barking and clattering were coming from the kitchen. Emily poked her head round the door of the studio and beckoned to him. 'Quick! While Mrs Roberts is still clearing up the mess!'

Scott hurried across to the studio and stood in the doorway, holding up the photograph. 'Look at this!' he hissed. 'Mrs Roberts *was* Anita Nesbitt in the Copycat Gang!'

Emily came to the door and looked at the photo. 'But that's *Laura* Roberts!'

'Just wait till you see this!' Jack shouted. Scott looked up to see his brother in the corner of the studio next to a large easel with an old blanket draped over it. Jack wasn't going to let Scott upstage his dramatic Moment of Truth. 'Ladies and gentlemen, I give you one perfect forgery of a world-famous Digory Trago masterpiece!' With all the flourish of a magician pulling a rabbit out of a hat, Jack whipped away the blanket.

He watched Emily and Scott's faces, waiting for their expressions of amazement. There was a long silence. Well, they *did* look amazed, but not in a good way. Scott blinked slowly. Emily gaped at the easel with her mouth open.

Jack looked down at the canvas.

There wasn't an animal orchestra in sight! No tuba-trunked elephants. No zebra-striped pianos.

Just a little girl running through a flower meadow.

Twelve

The Missing Piece of the Puzzle

'What are you doing?'

As one, Jack, Scott and Emily looked up from the easel to see Mrs Roberts in the studio doorway. The friends all shared the same thought: *How long has she been standing there, and how much has she heard?*

Mrs Roberts' eyes darted from the easel to the grey blanket lying on the floor to the newspaper photograph in Scott's hand. Her hands flew to her mouth and she took a step back. 'Where did you find that picture?'

Jack's brain whirred and clanked, trying to come up with an innocent explanation for why they were snooping around in the studio, and why Scott just happened to have a twenty-five-year-old newspaper photograph of Mrs Roberts in his hand. He'd been caught in some pretty tricky situations before, and he'd never yet failed to come up with an excuse, even if some of them were decidedly feeble. (*I was just testing the fire extinguisher to make sure it's still working,* sprang to mind.) But this time he was totally stumped. He looked at Scott and Emily. Even Emily was lost for words. *There's only one thing for it,* Jack thought. *Tell the truth. What's the worst that can happen?*

'You were a member of the Copycat Gang, weren't you?' he stated dramatically. He was about to add *Anita* for extra effect, but Mrs Roberts was already staggering backwards and clutching at the doorframe as if he'd stabbed her through the heart. Scott caught her as she crumpled to the floor.

'Er, was it something I said?' Jack asked. Emily shot him a look that told him this wasn't a good time for jokes. She and Scott helped Mrs Roberts to the sofa. 'I'll, er, make a cup of tea, shall I?' Jack offered. That's what they always did on telly when someone fainted.

By the time Jack returned to the living room, Mrs Roberts had come round. She took the mug and sipped. Then she grimaced. Jack knew you were meant to put sugar in tea for shock, but he hadn't been sure how much. Perhaps six spoons was too much?

Mrs Roberts took the photograph from Scott's hand and gazed at her younger self. She closed her eyes and leaned back against the sofa cushion for a long moment. Then she sighed. 'Yes, it's true. I *was* in the Copycat Gang.'

'And your real name isn't Jean Roberts, is it?' Scott asked gently. 'It's Samantha Burlington.'

Mrs Roberts nodded slowly, her eyes still closed.

'Samantha Burlington?' Emily asked, frowning at Scott. 'But that wasn't one of the women in the gang. I wrote the names down in my notebook: Anita Nesbitt and Rosie something.'

Mrs Roberts opened her eyes and turned to Emily. 'Scott's right. I *am* Samantha, but I went by the name Anita when I was working with the gang.'

Jack flopped down into an armchair. This was giving him brain-ache! How come *everyone* in this case had a selection of fake names to choose from? Bianca Mendez was really Nina Rodriguez. Mrs Roberts was Anita Nesbitt *and* Samantha Burlington! He wouldn't be surprised if Biscuit – who was sulking in his basket in the corner following the Great Sausage Incident – suddenly turned out to be called Gnasher or Foo-Foo or Cuthbert P. Fishgirdle!

'What happened?' Emily asked. 'How did you get involved with the gang in the first place?'

Mrs Roberts sighed again. 'I always wanted to be an artist. But my parents wanted me to marry a rich cousin and live in a big house in the country. When I ran away to London and enrolled at art college my whole family disowned me. But I was happy – even though I was living on next to nothing. A few months later I met a man at a student exhibition. He said he loved my work and that he had a job for me. The money he offered . . . well, I couldn't turn it down.'

'Juan Delgado?' Scott asked.

Mrs Roberts flinched when she heard the name. Then she nodded and sipped her tea again. She seemed to be getting used to the six sugars. 'At first it all seemed glamorous and exciting. I'd always found it easy to imitate other artists' styles, so painting the forgeries was no problem. But after a while I'd had enough. I had plenty of money to finish my course and I was afraid the police would catch up with us soon. I decided it was time to leave the gang.' Mrs Roberts sank her head in her hands. 'But when I told Delgado, he said if I ever tried to get away he would track me down and . . . well, it wasn't going to be pretty.' Mrs Roberts shuddered at the memory. Her voice had dwindled to a whisper. 'Not long after that, Nina told me Delgado had killed the last girl who tried to quit the gang. So I knew he was serious.'

'But you *did* leave?' Emily asked.

'Things got so bad Delgado was practically holding

me prisoner. One night we were at the lock-up where we kept the stolen paintings until they were sold on. Delgado got a phone call. A buyer was making trouble and threatening to go to the police. Delgado and his henchmen all rushed off to deal with the situation. I think they forgot I was there. I saw my chance and made a run for it. All I had was the cash in my handbag and . . .' Mrs Roberts paused, as if trying to decide how many layers of the onion she was prepared to peel back. Then she shrugged. There was no turning back now. '. . . and I took one of the stolen paintings too: Leonardo da Vinci's *Lady in Blue.*' She glanced up at the print on the wall. 'I thought it would be a kind of insurance policy. I could sell it if I got really desperate for money.'

Scott nodded. 'And then you came to Castle Key?'

'I changed my name, my appearance, everything. I was lucky enough to get the job at the school and I met Harry and got married. I heard Delgado and the other gang members all fled to South America. I thought I'd left my old life behind, that they'd never find me living here on this remote little island. And I was right – until last week, when Nina Rodriguez turned up on my doorstep.'

'But how did she find you after all this time?' Jack asked.

Mrs Roberts rose shakily to her feet, stumbled to the sideboard and picked up a photo of Laura – one of those school mug-shots that always look like Wanted posters.

Scott stared at the photo. Laura looked so like her mother did in the old newspaper photo that they could have been identical twins! And suddenly he knew the answer to Jack's question. The missing piece of the puzzle was the YouTube video! The one of the donkey mayhem at the fête! So that explained why Mrs Roberts had looked so terrified when they showed her the clip! It wasn't that she was a technophobe after all. She'd had every reason to be scared. She knew that Juan Delgado might see it – even in South America – and recognize Laura. Delgado would come looking for her. And, since Colin Warnock had entitled the clip *Donkey Demolition at Castle Key Fête*, he'd know just where to look. Except it hadn't been Delgado who saw the video, it had been Bianca.

Mrs Roberts hugged Laura's photo to her chest and sank back down onto the sofa. 'When you told me that video had been seen all over the world I knew I was in trouble. There was every chance someone from the gang would recognize Laura.'

'And they did,' Emily said. 'Bianca Mendez!'

'You mean Nina Rodriguez,' Jack chimed in, just to show he was keeping up.

Mrs Roberts nodded. 'Yes, she'd seen it. She left a comment on the clip to let me know. I saw it on your phone, Scott. Four simple words: *See you soon, Anita*. My past was back to haunt me! The only people who knew me as Anita were the other members of the

Copycat Gang. I thought Delgado was coming back to punish me, and to get back the painting I took when I ran away.'

'You mean you never sold it?' Jack asked, unable to hide his surprise.

Mrs Roberts sighed. 'No. I didn't need the money once I had my teaching job. And trying to find a buyer would have risked revealing my identity. In fact, I always intended to give it back to the gallery one day – anonymously, of course. But I was worried the police might trace it back to me. So in the end I just hung on to it.'

'But that painting's worth millions of pounds!' Jack whistled. 'You must have found an awesome hiding place for it.'

Behind her large glasses, Mrs Roberts' eyes flickered towards the fireplace. She smiled for the first time since her fainting fit. 'Yes,' she said. 'I did!'

she meant.

Thirteen

Doing the Right Thing

Emily followed Mrs Roberts' gaze. Could it be true? Did Mrs Roberts really mean what she thought she meant? 'The *Lady in Blue* you had hanging up there before? You're saying it was the *real thing*? The one the Copycat Gang stole from the gallery in London?'

Mrs Roberts took off her glasses, rubbed her eyes, and nodded. 'It seemed the safest place to keep it. Nobody expects to find an original da Vinci hanging on an ordinary living room wall. Everyone assumed it was a cheap print like all the others.'

'Genius!' Jack breathed. 'Until your house got broken into the other day, of course. Wow! I bet those burglars had no idea they'd got a priceless masterpiece on their hands. They probably just flogged it for a tenner in Carrickstowe Market or something!'

Suddenly there was a commotion. Mrs Roberts looked as if she was about to keel over again, as Biscuit did a vertical take-off out of his basket and threw himself at the window in a flurry of barking. From his position, curled up on Emily's feet, Drift raised one ear and sighed. Biscuit wasn't a bad little dude – and he'd taken the blame for the sausage incident on the chin – but he really needed to sort out his Territorial Alerts. Hadn't he heard of the dog who barked wolf? Even a *puppy* could hear that this was just the postman parking his bike by the garden gate and sliding letters through the door. Postmen had some sort of all-territory pass. You didn't need to bark at them.

Emily looked down at Drift's expression. If dogs could roll their eyes, that's what he'd be doing. She was suddenly reminded of the old puzzle about the burglary. *Why did nobody hear Biscuit barking when Lilac Cottage was broken into?* If the burglar was someone that Biscuit knew really well, it narrowed it down to Aunt Kate or Laura or . . . A light came on in Emily's brain, flickering into life like a candle flame.

'Mrs Roberts,' she said softly, 'there wasn't a break-in, was there?'

Jack and Scott gawped at her as if she'd claimed there was no such thing as chocolate ice cream. But Mrs Roberts looked up from cuddling Biscuit, who was now sitting on her lap, and slowly shook her head.

Emily turned to the boys and explained. 'When Mrs Roberts realized one of the gang members might see the video and come looking for her, she knew they might twig that the *Lady in Blue* on the wall was the original that went missing all those years ago. So she *pretended* it had been stolen and hid it somewhere else.'

Jack grinned. 'Phew! No wonder we couldn't find any clues in Operation Break-in. I thought we were just losing our touch.'

'But I needn't have bothered,' Mrs Roberts sighed. 'When Bianca turned up she wasn't after the *Lady in Blue*. She didn't even know I had it. She wanted me to help her steal another painting.'

'Not that Digory Trago one with all the animals playing weird instruments, by any chance?' Jack asked, as if he were taking a wild guess.

'The *Animal Orchestra*? Yes! You saw me studying it in the gallery, didn't you?' Mrs Roberts stared at the three friends as if she was waking from a hypnotic trance. 'But how did you find out about the Copycat Gang and Delgado?'

Emily explained Operation Copycat: how she'd

followed Bianca to the gallery, and then discovered her real name was Nina Rodriguez, and how they'd found the connection with the Copycat Gang on the internet. 'When we saw you studying the *Animal Orchestra*,' she concluded, 'we guessed that was the picture you and Bianca were planning to steal.'

'Yeah, awesome! Back together with your old partner in crime for one last big job!' Jack couldn't help looking at Mrs Roberts with a new respect now that he knew she had a secret identity as part of an international art theft ring. Well, maybe not a *ring* exactly, if it was just her and Bianca now – more of a duo! Did Mrs Roberts cast off her thick glasses and baggy cardigan when she was being Anita Nesbitt, he wondered, and change into a slinky outfit like Wonder Woman or Catwoman?

But Mrs Roberts shook her head. 'Not *awesome* at all. I didn't *want* to do it. Nina blackmailed me. She has a buyer lined up for the Trago painting – a billionaire collector in Amsterdam – and she wanted me to paint a copy so she could hang it in place of the original in the gallery.'

'Let me guess,' Scott said. 'She told you that if you didn't do it, she'd call Delgado and tell him exactly where to find you?'

Mrs Roberts shuddered. 'That's right. And – more importantly – where to find Laura. And I have no doubt she'll do it!'

'But you agreed to help her steal the Trago painting, so why would she tell him?' Emily asked.

Mrs Roberts got up and walked slowly to the door of the studio. She gazed towards her easel and out to the garden beyond, where the ashes of the bonfire were still smouldering. 'The thing is, I changed my mind. At first I was so frightened I agreed to everything. But Digory Trago was a friend of mine for over twenty years. The more I worked on the copy the more I realized I was betraying him – and artists everywhere – by faking his work.' She turned back from the studio with a trace of a smile. 'I am a retired teacher, after all. I've spent years telling my students that it's wrong to copy other people's work. Creativity is the most important thing. And taking responsibility for your own actions.'

'After I saw you three at the gallery,' Mrs Roberts went on, 'I came straight back and threw my half-finished copy of the *Animal Orchestra* on the bonfire. When Nina came to see how the copy was coming along this afternoon, I showed her the flames. She took one look and stormed out without a word. By now she'll have made her call to Delgado.' Mrs Roberts swallowed and pulled her cardigan round her as if speaking Delgado's name had chilled her to the bone.

Emily ran up to Mrs Roberts and put her arms round her. 'But what are you going to *do*? He'll come looking for you!'

Mrs Roberts glanced at her watch. 'Delgado lives in South America. At least that means he can't get here before the morning. By then I'll be long gone.

I've packed a few things.' She looked sadly round the room. 'I'll leave in the night and pick up Laura on the way. Poor Laura. She knows nothing about my past. It breaks my heart to have to drag her away from Castle Key, but I can't leave her here for Delgado to find. We'll start again and make a new life somewhere else. And poor Biscuit too.' Mrs Roberts stooped and picked up the little dog. 'It's going to be hard for him being on the road until we can settle down somewhere.' Her voice cracked and tears rolled down her face.

Emily could feel tears pricking her own eyes too. When she spoke she felt as if a tennis ball had lodged in her throat. 'I could have Biscuit for you. He could live with me and Drift at The Lighthouse.' She tried not to think of what Mum and Dad would say when she turned up with an extra dog – especially one that barked every time a seagull flew past – but she'd deal with that later!

Now Mrs Roberts was crying even more. 'Thank you, dear, but I couldn't bear to part with him. He's part of the family! We'll be fine.'

'We could at least try to delay Delgado somehow,' Scott offered.

Mrs Roberts shook her head. 'This isn't something you want to be mixed up in. Juan Delgado is a nasty piece of work. And, anyway, what I've done is *wrong*. I helped to steal all those paintings. I really ought to be telling you to go straight to the police and turn me in.'

Emily didn't know what to say. Of course, she knew that stealing was wrong and that Mrs Roberts had broken the law. But that was more than twenty years ago when she'd been very young and had got caught up with the wrong people. She'd never done anything wrong since. And she *had* refused to help Bianca steal the Trago painting.

Suddenly Mrs Roberts' face brightened. 'I've just thought of a way you *can* do the right thing and help me at the same time. That's if you're sure you want to?'

Emily, Scott and Jack exchanged excited looks. *Of course* they wanted to! Jack thought the Doing the Right Thing part sounded a bit tedious – like volunteering to help tidy up the classroom or something – but if it involved helping a secret art forger escape from a ruthless international criminal gang-leader, he'd be the first to put his hand up!

Fourteen

A Dangerous Visitor

As they left Lilac Cottage, the friends couldn't wait to get back to their HQ to talk over the astonishing story Mrs Roberts had told them – and, of course, her request for their help.

Jack had the brainwave of asking Aunt Kate if they could take a picnic tea up to the tree house, and soon they were hoisting sandwiches and pork pies and crisps and chocolate cake and a big bottle of apple juice up to the platform in Drift's basket – not forgetting a bowl of water and some dog biscuits, of course. They spread a tablecloth on the platform, laid out their feast and made themselves comfortable on the cushions.

'Poor Mrs Roberts,' Emily sighed. 'If I had to leave The Lighthouse and Castle Key, I don't know what I'd do.'

Jack nodded and took a big bite of pork pie. 'She'll have to pick *another* new name for a start! I wonder what she'll go for this time. Ermintrude Bagshot?' He laughed. 'If I had to change my identity I'd go for something epic like Flash Maverick or Storm Deadlock.'

Scott rolled his eyes. Trust Jack to start making up stupid names when Emily was trying to be serious! His brother had the emotional maturity of a jelly baby! He'd obviously forgotten how miserable they'd both felt leaving their friends behind in London and coming to Castle Key – and that was only for a couple of months. Scott was suddenly sideswiped by the knowledge that he was going to feel just as sad when it was time to say goodbye to Castle Key and head back to London at the end of the summer. To help shake off the feeling, he threw a grape at Jack. 'Storm Deadlock? You look more like a Percival Primpsworthy to me!'

Jack returned fire with a cherry tomato. 'Bullseye!' he shouted as it splatted Scott on the nose.

'Can you two stop acting like baboons for one

minute?' Emily sighed. 'We've got some vital planning to do.' The food-fight showed no sign of stopping. Emily blew up a crisp packet and popped it with a bang. That got their attention!

'What are you trying to do?' Jack laughed, wrestling the packet out of Emily's hand. 'Give me a heart attack?'

'I thought for a minute that Juan Delgado had turned up and was using us for target practice!' Scott laughed.

Emily ignored them. 'We need to talk about *this*!' She held up a sealed envelope. The words *For the Attention of Detective Inspector Hassan, Carrickstowe Police Station* were written on the front in Mrs Roberts' neat teacher's handwriting. 'Mrs Roberts asked us to wait at least forty-eight hours after she'd gone before we go and retrieve the original *Lady in Blue* from its new hiding place and hand it over to the police with this letter of explanation. It's Wednesday now. I suggest we go and get the painting on Friday night.'

'Oh, I wanted to go *tonight*!' Jack grumbled, pouting like a toddler who's been told he can't go to the park.

'Emily's right,' Scott said. 'We need to give Mrs Roberts and Laura time to get well away from here, and Delgado time to give up the search and ship off back to South America. That's if he *does* come looking. Maybe after all this time he'll have got over it and moved on.'

Emily took her notebook out of her bag and slid the

envelope inside. 'I've got all the instructions written down here.'

'It's so cool that Mrs Roberts has hidden the *Lady in Blue* in the Trago Gallery!' Jack said. 'I can't wait to find the secret entrance she told us about.'

Scott took a handful of crisps. For once he agreed with his brother. He couldn't wait either! Only a few of Digory Trago's friends knew about the secret entrance, Mrs Roberts had told them. She knew about it because she used to help Trago in his studio and they'd become quite close in the last few years of his life. The entrance was so secret it hadn't even been wired up to the alarm when the security system was installed. With Mrs Roberts' detailed instructions, the friends could sneak into the gallery at night, retrieve the *Lady in Blue* from her hiding place, and sneak back out again without anyone knowing anything about it. 'And then we do the right thing! Hand the painting in to the police along with the letter,' Scott said.

'I suppose we *do* have to hand it in?' Jack asked. 'Because I still quite fancy that private plane I didn't get when you guys wouldn't let me keep the hidden gold from Gulliver's Island.'

'Jack, you're not really suggesting we try to find a buyer for the *Lady in Blue*?' Scott snorted. 'You know a lot about the black market for stolen Leonardo da Vinci masterpieces, do you? And old Delgado will be after you . . .'

'Not to mention that it would be *stealing*!' Emily added firmly.

Suddenly Drift pricked up his ears. He'd heard something from his vantage point, lying on the platform on Lookout Duty. He trotted to Emily and alerted her with one short, soft bark, which translated as: *You might be interested in having a look at this.*

The friends peeked out through the leaves. A black car had pulled up outside Lilac Cottage. Inside the house, Biscuit could be heard, working himself up into his usual yap-athon. A tall man got out of the car and stood for a moment looking up and down Church Lane. His face was tanned but the stubble that shadowed his jaw was grey and there was a white streak running through his thick black hair. His white shirt and cream chino trousers were smart but crumpled. This man had clearly been travelling.

Scott turned to Jack and Emily. 'Juan Delgado?'

They both nodded.

'How'd he get here that fast from South America?' Jack gasped. 'A teleporter?'

'He must have been somewhere in Europe already,' Scott said.

Emily was already scrambling down the rope ladder. 'Mrs Roberts is still there! She's in danger!'

Moments later, Scott, Emily and Jack were crouching among the rose bushes below the studio window at the back of Lilac Cottage. The window was open a crack.

113

Scott craned his neck and peeped over the sill.

Delgado was standing with his arms folded, calmly studying the painting of the little girl in the flower meadow on the easel. 'Hmmm. Not bad,' he murmured. 'But rather sentimental.'

'Please leave me alone!' Mrs Roberts was cowering in the doorway behind him. 'I don't have the *Lady in Blue* any more!'

'Try again, Anita!' Delgado's quiet voice throbbed with power and menace. 'I can tell you're lying.'

'I told you!' Mrs Roberts sobbed. 'It was stolen a few days ago. I had a burglary. You can check with the police!'

Delgado sauntered towards the window with his hands in his pockets. A cold hard fact suddenly dawned on Scott: *We could be in a world of danger here. If Delgado catches us listening at the window who knows what he'll do?* One thing was for sure. He didn't look like the kind of guy to pat them on the head and tell them to run off home and keep out of mischief. Leaving the country and living under a new identity would be the least of their worries. Scott held his breath and tried to blend in with the rosebush – even though its sabre-like thorns were tearing the skin from his arms. Delgado gazed through the window at the garden and then turned back to Mrs Roberts. Scott allowed himself to breathe again.

'You might want to reconsider that answer, Anita.'

Delgado reached into his pocket and pulled out his mobile phone. 'My man at the riding stables says that you have a *very* pretty daughter . . .' His voice was cruelly casual.

Mrs Roberts ran across the studio and grasped his hand. 'What have you done with Laura? You leave her alone!'

Delgado smiled and brushed her away as if she were a bothersome fly. 'Laura will be perfectly safe. As long as you co-operate, of course. Show me where you've hidden the *Lady in Blue* and I will tell Carlo to release her!' He held up the phone and contemplated it for a long moment. 'If you *don't* . . .' Delgado shook his head as if the thought saddened him deeply, 'well, it's up to you . . .'

'Alright!' Mrs Roberts was almost screaming now. 'I'll show you. Just promise you won't hurt her!' With that she ran into the living room. Delgado strolled after her with a lizard-like smile playing across his lips. 'Oh, and Anita,' he called after her, 'don't even think of trying to raise the alarm. I have Carlo on speed dial.'

The friends crept to the side of the house and peeped round the corner in time to see Delgado leading Mrs Roberts out through the gate towards his car. Holding her by the arm, he smiled as if at a joke they were sharing. If any neighbours happened to be looking on they'd think Mrs Roberts was going out for the evening with a handsome new friend. But Scott saw how tightly Delgado was gripping her elbow and heard his chilling words.

'One tiny little wave or cry for help, Anita, and you will *never* see your daughter again. Do I make myself clear?'

Fifteen

We Need a Plan!

Emily jumped out from behind the wall and watched Delgado's car cruise off down Church Lane. 'We've got to call the police!'

Scott reached for his phone but Jack grabbed his arm. 'Are you off your head? You heard that Delgado bloke. If the police turn up, he'll just tell his mate Carlo to bump Laura off.'

Scott slid his phone back into his jeans pocket. 'I

117

never thought I'd say this, but Jack has a point.'

Emily nodded and sighed. 'But we can't just let Delgado walk off with that priceless painting!'

Scott leaned against the wall. He'd seen Delgado's face when he promised not to hurt Laura if Mrs Roberts co-operated. He'd looked about as sincere as a weasel in a nest of baby chicks. 'I don't trust Delgado to keep his word. He'll probably kill Laura even if he *does* get the painting.' He kicked out in frustration at a clump of geraniums. 'We've got to do *something*. I just don't know what!'

'We need a plan!' Emily tugged at her hair. 'Think! *Think!*'

But Jack was already running towards Stone Cottage to fetch his bike. 'Come on! We don't have time for *plans*! Let's get up to the gallery before Mr Nasty nabs the painting and disappears. We'll just have to wing it when we get there!'

Emily hesitated. It was true; there was no time to hang about. But if they were going to stop Delgado getting away with the masterpiece without putting Laura's life at risk they were going to have to come up with something better than *winging it*! They were going to have to outwit him somehow. Suddenly she had an idea. 'Wait!' she yelled at Jack. She ran into Lilac Cottage – Mrs Roberts had left the front door unlocked when Delgado dragged her off. 'Quick, help me get the *Lady in Blue* down,' she shouted to Scott who had hurried in after her.

Scott took the print down from its hook on the wall. Emily threw it onto the sofa and began frantically unclipping the frame from the backing board.

'What are you doing?' Scott asked.

'If we can get to the gallery before Delgado,' Emily said breathlessly as she worked, 'we can sneak in through that secret door Mrs Roberts told us about and switch the real *Lady in Blue* she hid in there for *this* one. But we've got to get the print out of the frame and roll the canvas up like a scroll. That's what Mrs Roberts said she'd done with the real one.'

'But won't Delgado *notice* this isn't the original?' Scott asked.

Emily had to admit that was a possibility, but the print had been deliberately made to look authentic – as if it was painted on old canvas – and, with luck, Delgado would be in such a hurry to get away before the alarm was raised, he wouldn't look too closely. It had to be worth a try. 'If Delgado thinks he's got the original, he might just leave Mrs Roberts and Laura alone – at least long enough for them to get away from Castle Key before he finds out the truth.'

'Sounds good to me!' Jack's voice from the doorway made Emily jump. 'Chuck me that painting and I'll go on ahead. I'm much faster on my bike than you slowcoaches.'

'OK,' Emily said. 'We'll meet you there. Cut through the churchyard and take the footpath straight over the headland. Delgado will have to go all the way round by the road in the car. You should get there before him. Can you remember the instructions for the secret entrance? And the hiding place?'

Jack rolled his eyes and snorted. 'Do I *look* stupid?' He caught the rolled-up print as if it was a rugby ball, and dashed out of the door.

Scott turned to Emily and shrugged. 'Yeah, he *does*! That's the part I'm worried about.' He hesitated, then ran outside and leaned over the garden gate. Jack was heading down Church Lane, standing up on the pedals of his BMX bike, his legs pumping like a manic clockwork monkey. 'If you see Delgado's car there already, the plan's off!' Scott shouted after the receding figure. 'You stay outside and wait for us! No stupid heroics, OK?' He watched as his brother punched the air, his bike swerving wildly as he made for the churchyard gate.

As they pushed their bikes out into the lane, Scott couldn't help worrying. If Delgado got wind that there was some kind of trickery going on, he only had to make one call and Laura's life would be in danger. He put his hand on Emily's shoulder. 'You go up to the gallery and meet Jack. Delgado said his man was holding Laura at the riding stables. I'll go there and see if I can find out what's happening. I'll call you and report on the situation. Just don't let Jack try and tackle Delgado with some kind of mad Pink Panther-style ambush or anything!'

Emily nodded seriously as Drift hopped into the basket on the back of her bike.

Scott watched Emily pedal away. 'Good luck, Em!' he called.

'You too! Oh, and Scott!' she called back over her shoulder. 'No stupid heroics, OK?'

Scott was about to set off for Roshendra Farm when he heard a rustle under a lilac bush next to the garden gate. A black nose peeped out from the undergrowth. 'Drift! I thought you were with Emily!' he murmured. But when the dog attached to the nose appeared, it wasn't Drift. It was *Biscuit*!

The little terrier was trembling. He opened his mouth but only a feeble croak squeaked out.

'Poor little chap!' Scott said. 'Did you get left behind? You're going to have to stay here a bit longer, I'm afraid.'

Biscuit licked his hand.

'No, I can't take you with me.'

Biscuit gazed up at him with big melting eyes.

'No, I can't! Oh, alright!' Scott bundled Biscuit into his backpack and zipped it up just far enough so that his head poked out of the top. 'Let's go!'

—

Scott was turbo-pedalling along the road that led north out of Castle Key before cutting across the moors to Roshendra Farm. He checked his watch. *Should be there in ten minutes, tops.* He just had to hope that Delgado's accomplice, Carlo, was still keeping Laura at the riding stables and hadn't moved her to another location.

Scott was so focused on the mission at hand, he didn't see the group of lads gathered at the side of the road, spray-painting graffiti on the side of an old barn. He almost ploughed straight into them, swerving at the last minute and falling off his bike in an untidy – and embarrassingly uncool – heap.

'Watch what you're doing!' A wiry dark-haired boy of about seventeen swaggered towards Scott, hands deep in the pockets of black skinny jeans. The way he positioned himself at the front of the pack told Scott he was the leader.

'Ooh, look, it's that *London boy* Emily Wild's been hanging out with!' a beefy guy with fierce red curls said with a sneer.

The leader stepped forward, giving Scott a close-up of his spots, dyed black hair and nose-rings. 'Who do you think you are, anyway?'

Scott got to his feet and brushed himself down with as much dignity as he could muster. He didn't want to get into a fight – there were five of them and only one of him – and he didn't have time for a philosophical debate about who he thought he was. He glanced around for an escape route. The graffiti on the old barn wall was glistening still with wet paint. The metre-high letters in orange, white and blue were familiar: *AM-EN. What*

did Emily say the AM-EN guy's name was? Adam
Something. Martin? Yes, that was it. And the other four
must be the Extreme Network!

'You're Adam Martin?' he asked.

Adam eyed Scott suspiciously. 'Yeah, what's it to you?'

Scott shrugged. 'I recognized your tag. It's cool.'

Adam still looked doubtful.

Suddenly Scott remembered Emily saying that Adam Martin hadn't broken into Lilac Cottage because Mrs Roberts was his favourite teacher. That gave him an idea. Maybe instead of just trying to shake these guys off as fast as possible, he should get them on his side. They could help scope out what was happening with Laura. 'There's a great Street Art group where I live,' Scott said. 'I could tell them about your stuff. Maybe you could come up to London and work on some projects with them.'

Adam dropped the scowl and looked mildly interested. 'Oh, yeah? London?' He narrowed his eyes and chewed his gum for a moment, then took a step back out of Scott's personal space.

Scott decided it was time to strike. 'Look, thing is I need your help!' He explained as quickly as he could that Mrs Roberts and her daughter were in serious trouble, and that he was on his way to the stables. 'So, d'you guys want to come with me and cause a distraction to get the guard out of the way for a minute? Then I can slip in and do a recce – see if there's a way to get Laura out . . .'

Adam Martin stared at Scott for a long moment, as if he suspected him of winding him up. But then he shrugged. 'OK, you're on. It's not like our social diaries are exactly packed with other offers.'

'Yeah, nothing ever happens round here,' the guy with the red curls grouched.

'One *distraction* coming right up!' Adam grinned at the others and they all laughed. Then he turned back to Scott. 'But you'll have to ditch that naff push-bike, Scotto mate!'

Scott hid his bike down the side of the barn and climbed onto the back of Adam's moped. He wasn't sure that inviting the Extreme Network along was the best idea he'd ever had, but at least he'd get to the stables faster this way.

'Hold on!' Adam yelled, revving the small engine to within an inch of its life and accelerating so hard the front wheel reared up like a wild stallion.

A lot faster! Scott thought. *If we actually make it there in one piece!*

Sixteen

Through the Secret Entrance

Meanwhile, Emily had reached the Trago Gallery and was waiting for Jack outside the secret entrance at the back of the building. The car park was empty. All the staff and visitors had left long ago and it seemed that Delgado had not yet arrived.

Emily checked her watch. Jack must have been inside at least five minutes. Surely that was plenty of time to do the switch and get out? Delgado and Mrs Roberts

125

would be here any second. Another minute ticked past. 'What's he *doing* in there, Drift?' she asked.

Drift's ears drooped. He didn't know either.

I should never have trusted Jack to do this on his own, Emily thought. *He's probably forgotten where the hiding place is!*

Another twenty seconds crawled past. Emily checked her phone. There was nothing from Scott either. 'It's no good, Drift,' she sighed. 'We're going to have to go in and find Jack before Delgado gets here.' She took her notebook from her bag and re-read the instructions for the secret entrance. She climbed the stairs to a small balcony. Yes, this was the place. There was the false doorway. It was so realistic Emily had to run her fingers over the bricks to convince herself it was painted onto the wall. The only thing that was real was the big brass doorknob in the middle.

The floor of the balcony was paved with brightly coloured tiles arranged in the shape of a snail. All you had to do was sit down in the middle of the spiral pattern of the snail's shell, then reach out and turn the doorknob on the wall three times anti-clockwise. It was important to be sitting down, Mrs Roberts had explained, because the snail shell would slide open and you'd be flying down a giant chute into the cellar.

Emily sat down cross-legged with Drift on her lap. 'OK, here goes. Hold on tight!' She reached for the doorknob on the wall. And reached. *And reached.* Her fingers closed on nothing but the warm evening air. Emily banged her fists down on the snail shell. She remembered seeing Digory Trago around the village before he died. He shuffled with a stick and he liked to team a kilt of yellow and black Cornish tartan with a black velvet jacket. More importantly, *he was well over six feet tall.* He'd obviously not been catering for anyone as small as Emily when he designed this secret entrance! Even when she stood up and stretched as far as she could, she still couldn't reach the doorknob. And she couldn't just move closer, because the entrance needed the weight on the centre of the snail shell to trigger the opening mechanism.

Emily looked around the balcony. There *had* to be a way to get around this. But there were no extendable arms or magic growth potions in sight. She and Drift were going to have to work as a team. It might work if Drift was heavy enough . . .

'Stay!' she said, putting Drift in the correct position.

Drift sat neatly on the central tile, tucked in his tail and awaited further instructions. Emily crawled closer to the wall, grasped the doorknob, took a deep breath and turned it – once, twice, three times . . . On the third turn she threw herself sideways to land on top of Drift – just in time to fall through the hole as the tiles slid apart with a well-oiled hiss. Drift yelped with surprise as they careened down a helter-skelter slide, round and round, faster and faster, in a tangle of arms, legs, paws, hair and fur. By the time they shot out and bounced onto a squashy landing area, Emily no longer knew where she ended and Drift began.

There was a whirring sound as the chute wound itself back up into the ceiling. Emily sat up and looked at Drift. He was panting, with his tongue hanging out, and doing his Eager Ears. He wanted to do it again!

'Maybe another day!' Emily laughed, ruffling his fur. 'Right now, we've got to find out what Jack's doing.'

What Jack was doing at that moment was getting hopelessly lost! And it had all *started* so well. He'd cracked the whole snail-and-doorknob combo first time. And, wow, that chute was awesome! He'd have gone straight back out for another go – if he'd known *how* to get back out. Mrs Roberts had told them about the secret entrance. As far as Jack could recall, she'd not mentioned anything about a secret *exit*! But that was the least of his worries. First he had to find this stupid hiding place and do the switcheroony.

The flying pig! That's where Mrs Roberts had told them she'd hidden the *Lady in Blue*! Jack knew exactly where she meant, of course. He'd noticed the life-sized porker – complete with sparkly wings and a tiara – hanging from the ceiling in the entrance hall when they visited the Trago Gallery earlier. Well, it wasn't the kind of thing you could easily miss!

Find the flying pig. How hard could it be? Well, *pretty hard*, as it turned out. First he had to find the entrance hall. The snail-slide had dropped him in a basement. He'd run up the first staircase he came to, but what with the false doors and the fake floors and the trick staircases and the dead ends, he'd found himself wandering round in circles. And then there were the surreal sculptures and giant stuffed animals, not to mention the fact that Juan Delgado might appear around the next corner at any moment. Scott's words rang in his ears. *No stupid heroics!* Huh! Fat chance of that happening! He was going to spend the rest of his natural life roaming this madhouse with a rolled-up painting stuffed in his shorts pocket. He'd had nightmares that made more sense than this!

It didn't help that it was half dark, with only the late evening light shining through the windows and the occasional emergency lamp to see by. Of course, *Emily* would have packed a torch! No doubt she'd have a compass and a satnav and an Automatic Flying Pig Detector too.

But I'm not Emily ... I'm— Agggghhh! A hideous mutant gnome! It's coming straight at me! Jack dived behind a group of stegosaurus skeletons, heart pounding against his ribcage.

He peeped out from behind the stegosauruses. The

gnome was just *standing* there staring at him from the shadows. It was only three feet high and almost as wide, with stumpy legs and a flat, pale face. Jack waited and then took a cautious step. So did the gnome. Jack took another step. So did the gnome. Then Jack slapped his forehead and laughed out loud. And so did the gnome. 'It's a distorting mirror!' Jack gasped, laughing with relief. 'You haven't seen any flying pigs round here, have you mate?' he asked his reflection.

And that's when he heard footsteps. He spun round but there was no one behind him. It was impossible to tell where the steps were coming from in this crazy twisted building. *It must be Delgado!*

His skin crawling with fear, Jack began backing slowly away from the mirrors – straight into someone reversing in the opposite direction.

Seventeen

The Hiding Place

'Agghh!'

Jack froze in terror. But wait! That wasn't the cry of a cold-blooded South American criminal mastermind. And that wasn't the friendly lick on the knee of a cold-blooded South American criminal mastermind's dog either! *It was Emily and Drift.* He hadn't felt so relieved since Simon Fox's bullet had whizzed past his left ear.

'You stood on my toe, you great *elephant*!' Emily snapped, hopping around clutching her flip-flopped foot. 'I've been looking for you for ages. You've swapped the paintings, right?'

Jack shook his head. He didn't trust himself to speak yet. After the fright he'd just had, he had a feeling his voice would come out as a helium-balloon squeak.

Emily clapped her hands to the sides of her head and did a silent scream of despair. 'So what on earth,' she asked, 'are you doing all the way up here? You're miles from the pig. And why were you mucking around talking to yourself in the mirror?'

Jack opened his mouth, wondering whether he could come up with a story that didn't involve admitting he'd mistaken his reflection for a mutant gnome (if Scott ever found out, his life wouldn't be worth living). But Emily wasn't hanging around to listen to explanations anyway.

'Come on,' she snapped, pulling him by the arm. 'We've got to switch these paintings before Delgado turns up.'

'Where's Scott?' Jack puffed as they raced off up a winding staircase.

'Riding stables,' Emily said. 'I'll explain later.'

'And how come you know your way round this place?'

'Guidebook!' Emily waved a book at him. 'I picked

it up when we were here this morning. It's got a map and everything.'

Jack stopped dead halfway up the stairs. 'You mean you had a *map* and you didn't bother to mention it to me! I could have died of starvation wandering around this place!'

Emily turned to look down at Jack from the top of the stairs. 'Er, yeah, sorry about that. But you zoomed off on your bike so fast I didn't have a chance.'

After twisting and turning their way through the maze, Emily, Drift and Jack eventually came out at the top of the grand staircase in the hall. They crouched down and peeped through the posts of the banister. The hall, with its pillars and mirrors and black-and-white-tiled sloping floor, was empty.

The friends tiptoed down the stairs, past a stuffed grizzly bear standing guard on a small landing. Moments later they were in the hall looking up into the beady black eyes of a pig, suspended from the ceiling on long chains.

'Mrs Roberts said she'd hidden the painting inside the pig's mouth,' Emily said.

'Right, and we open her mouth by pulling on her tail.' Jack was glad that he'd been listening, for once. 'I'm guessing she's a *girl* pig with that tiara.'

Emily wasn't listening. She was too busy pulling over a chair to stand on. Although it was a low-flying pig – a tall man would have to duck to avoid being struck by a stray trotter as he passed beneath it – Emily couldn't reach it. She was starting to bear a grudge against anyone over five feet tall.

'Quick!' She breathed. 'Pull the tail. Delgado will be here any second!'

Jack grabbed the tail and gave it a tug. The pig's bottom jaw dropped down with a clunk. Emily climbed on the chair, stretched up and put her hand into the gaping mouth. To her relief the model wasn't made out of a real pig's body: it was papier-mâché over a wire frame. She felt around. Her hand brushed against the frayed edge of a roll of canvas.

'I've got it! Catch!' She pulled the painting out and threw it to Jack. *Wow!* she thought. *I've just lobbed Jack a masterpiece worth millions of pounds as if it were an old frisbee!* That was surreal, even by Digory Trago's standards! But there was no time to worry about details! They had to get out before they were caught in the act. 'Hand me the print!'

Jack took the rolled-up print of the *Lady in Blue* from his shorts pocket, and held it up next to the original. He jiggled them up and down as if weighing them in his hands. 'Thirty million quid or thirty quid from Carrickstowe Art Shop? Take your pick.'

'Do you *want* Delgado to find us here?' Emily hissed.

Jack passed up the copy.

Emily snatched it and stuffed it in the pig's jaws. She couldn't wait to get out of the hall. But then she hesitated, one foot still on the chair. 'You are *sure* you gave me the right one, aren't you? That *was* the print?'

'Of course I'm sure. I've got thirty million smackers here!' Jack held up the rolled canvas. 'That's got to be enough for a private plane.'

'Shhh!' Emily whispered. 'Drift's heard something!'

Drift was looking towards the front door, his ears standing up and swivelling like satellite dishes.

'I can't hear anything,' Jack murmured.

'Shut it!' Emily hissed.

'No need to be like that!'

'No! Shut the *pig's* mouth!' Emily sighed. 'Drift's never wrong. A car just pulled up outside.'

As they hurtled up the stairs, Emily heard footsteps in the hall and glanced back over her shoulder. Her heart almost stopped beating. Delgado and Mrs Roberts were in the hall already! Delgado *must* have seen them. But, there he was again on the other side of the room. And again. Now there were hundreds of Delgados and hundreds of Mrs Roberts!

'It's the mirrors!' Jack gasped. 'Come on!' And with that he grabbed Emily's arm and they threw themselves headlong behind the grizzly bear on the landing.

—

Jack, Emily and Drift clung together and held their breath. Had Delgado seen them running away? Would he come after them? Were their lives about to end? Moments passed. It seemed their luck was in. They hadn't been seen!

Slowly Emily peeked out from behind the bear's tawny fur. Juan Delgado and Mrs Roberts were standing beneath the flying pig. Delgado watched, hands on hips, as Mrs Roberts pulled the tail, then reached into the pig's mouth and took out the rolled-up painting.

Delgado held his hand out and Mrs Roberts passed it to him. He unfurled the canvas a little. Emily held her breath. She looked at Jack with wide, frightened eyes. *Would Delgado spot the switch?* The light in the hall was dim, with long dark shadows. Delgado held the canvas up to catch the fading twilight from a high window. He looked at Mrs Roberts, who was hunched over with her head down, then he smiled and nodded. He slowly rolled the canvas back into a scroll and slid it into his black leather shoulder bag. 'Good! Good!' he murmured.

'Yes!' Emily said under her breath.

Jack grinned at her and made a thumbs-up sign.

'So, you'll call your man now and tell him to let Laura go?' Mrs Roberts pleaded in a shaky voice.

Suddenly Emily remembered that she hadn't checked her phone for texts or missed calls since she came into the gallery. Had Scott tried to call to report on the situation at the riding stables? But her phone was at the bottom of her bag; there was no way she could extract it without making a sound and giving away their position.

'Ah, yes, the lovely Laura!' Delgado said with a mocking smile. 'I'm not sure you really deserve my forgiveness after you double-crossed me. Running off like that with my painting. Most inconsiderate!'

'That was twenty-five years ago. And you *promised*!' Mrs Roberts begged. 'Please don't go back on your word.'

Delgado took his phone out of his pocket and switched it on. He laughed and the sound echoed round the hall. 'You see, Anita, earlier I wrote two text messages for Carlo. One says LIVE and the other says DIE. All I have to do is decide which one to send, and with one click the deed is done. As you've kept your side of the bargain, and we're old friends, I think I'll go for . . . LIVE!'

Mrs Roberts' entire body sagged with relief. 'Thank you!' she sobbed.

Emily gulped and smiled at Jack. Delgado had kept his word, after all. *Laura was safe!*

Delgado's thumb hovered over the keypad.

'Not so fast, Juan!'

Delgado and Mrs Roberts both whipped round to see where the voice had come from.

Bianca Mendez was striding across the hall, accompanied by hundreds of reflections.

And every single one of them was pointing a pistol at Juan Delgado's chest.

Eighteen

A Good Evening's Work

B ianca Mendez, alias Nina Rodriguez, alias – at least
in Jack's mind – Cruella de Vil, was dressed in black
trousers and shirt and had a black tubular case slung
over her shoulder. The small silver gun glinted in the
glow of the security light. Her forefinger – with its long,
pink-varnished nail – was curled around the trigger.

There was a long moment of silence supercharged
with tension. Delgado regarded Bianca, one eyebrow

raised. Bianca held the gun steady, her eyes flicking back and forth between Delgado and Mrs Roberts. Mrs Roberts stared at the phone in Delgado's hand. From Jack's position behind the bear on the landing, the three figures in the hall looked like characters in a computer game. If only he could press a key to make Mrs Roberts leap up and take out both Bianca and Delgado with a flying roundhouse kick.

Without letting the gun waver from Delgado, Bianca pulled the strap on the tubular case further up onto her shoulder and took a step closer.

What has she got in that tube? Jack wondered. *A telescope? A machine gun? I could do with one of those for carrying this rolled-up painting around.* Then he got it! Bianca had been in the main gallery nicking the Trago painting! She'd obviously decided to go ahead with her plan even without having Mrs Roberts' copy of the picture to hang in its place. That explained why she'd suddenly popped out from behind the mirrors! 'She's got the *Animal Orchestra* in that tube,' he mouthed to Emily.

Emily nodded. *Of course*, Jack thought, *Emily had figured that out ages ago!*

They both turned back to the scene in the hall as Bianca spoke. 'Well, how nice! A little reunion party for the Copycat Gang. I hope you don't mind me gate-crashing!'

Delgado held his hands out and took a step. 'Nina! Why don't you put that gun down?'

Bianca gestured with the gun and he shuffled back. 'What do you want?' Delgado asked.

'Well, let's see now.' Bianca pretended to give the question some serious thought. 'How about the *Lady in Blue* that you've got hidden in your bag?'

Delgado and Mrs Roberts gaped at her in surprise.

'Oh, yes,' Bianca laughed. 'I've been watching this little game for a few minutes now. I saw you take the canvas out of that pig.' She turned to Mrs Roberts. 'So, Anita, how interesting that you never mentioned that you'd kept the da Vinci painting. I thought you'd have sold that on years ago. Thought you'd rather team up with Juan, did you, and cut me out, you double-crossing little . . .'

Mrs Roberts shook her head. 'No, Nina, it's not like that. He threatened my daughter!'

Bianca laughed. 'Well, much as I'd like to stay and chat, time is running out. So, if you'll just hand over the da Vinci, I'll be on my way. Slide the bag across the floor. *Now*!'

Delgado lowered the bag to the floor and nudged it across the black and white tiles with his foot. Bianca crouched down, snagged the bag and slung it over her shoulder.

'That was a good evening's work, eh? A real two-for-one deal. I came for a Trago painting worth a piffling five million,' she patted the tubular case, 'and I got a da Vinci thrown in!'

That's what you think! Jack thought. What he wouldn't give to see Bianca's face when she realized her bonus gift was a thirty quid print!

'Well, goodbye Juan, Anita!' Bianca blew them each a kiss as she backed towards the door, the gun still trained on Delgado.

Emily watched with a feeling of dread growing in her chest like a cold, wet sponge. Delgado was going to be so furious he'd lost the *Lady in Blue* to Bianca that he was hardly going to be in the mood to call Carlo and tell him to release Laura now.

Suddenly Drift's ears flicked up into Listening Position again. Emily stroked his head, wondering what he'd heard. She didn't have to wait long to find out.

There was a cry of *'Freeze! Nobody move!'* as the front door burst open and an army of police officers charged in. At least, it *looked* like an army. In fact, Emily realized, it was four officers, multiplied over and over by their reflections in the mirrors. She didn't know where to look first: at Mrs Roberts and Delgado standing under the flying pig, at the police officers, who'd now been joined by the familiar bulky figure of Detective Inspector Hassan, or at Bianca Mendez . . .

Emily did a double take. *Bianca had vanished!*

D.I. Hassan barked an order to two of the officers. 'Go after her!' The two men jogged towards the mirrors. They hesitated for a moment as they tried to find the real door among the kaleidoscope of reflections; then they disappeared from sight.

Meanwhile D.I. Hassan flicked on all the lights in the room and the two remaining police officers approached Deglado, one of them pulling a pair of handcuffs from his belt.

Delgado watched them with an amused sneer. 'I suggest you back off!' he said in an icy monotone. He held up his mobile phone and waggled his thumb. 'One press and Laura Roberts will be killed!'

'Nooooo!' Mrs Roberts screamed, collapsing to her knees.

'What?' Emily spluttered, grabbing for Jack's arm as he thrust the rolled-up masterpiece into her hands and dived out from behind the bear. But she was too late.

She watched in horror as Jack leaped over the banister and plummeted towards Delgado's shoulders.

Nineteen

Scott to the Rescue

W hile Emily, Jack and Drift were at the Trago Gallery, Scott and Biscuit had arrived at Roshendra Farm riding stables. Scott had persuaded Adam Martin and the Extreme Network to park their mopeds and wait a little way off down the road while Scott approached the stables on foot. 'When I'm ready for the distraction,' he said, entering Adam's number into his phone, 'I'll text you the word GO. OK?'

'Sweet!' Adam held out his fist for a knuckle-touch. The rest of the crew did the same. Scott wasn't sure how, but it seemed he'd been made an honorary member of the Extreme Network.

Scott ran the rest of the way to the riding stables, keeping to the shadows of the hedgerow. The place was deserted and there were no lights on at the big farmhouse – the White family must be out for the evening. Scott ducked down behind the wall next to the gate. A few of the stables had the top halves of their doors open. Scott recognized the two donkeys, Wallace and Gromit, gazing out of the loose-box that they shared. Piper, the piebald pony, whickered softly.

Instead of going into the yard, Scott crept round the back of the stable block. He looked up at the tiny ventilation windows. To his excitement there was a dim light glowing through the window of the third stable along. Could Carlo be holding Laura hostage in there?

The little window was high up under the stable roof. Scott looked around for something to stand on so he could peep in. He spotted a stack of plastic blocks and poles used for constructing jumps. Working as swiftly and as quietly as he could, he dragged a block into place. Every little noise seemed to boom out in the still night air. Scott's heart was pounding in his ears. *Carlo will hear me at any moment. He'll come running out and . . .* Scott didn't let himself finish that thought. But at last the block was in place and he clambered onto it.

This would be a whole lot easier if I didn't have a dog in my backpack! Biscuit was starting to feel more like a Great Dane than a terrier! But when he'd tried to leave Biscuit with Adam, the little dog had started barking at the top of his voice. Scott was his new best friend and the only way to keep him quiet was for Scott to carry him around!

Scott put his eye to the small dusty pane of glass. He saw straw on the floor, a feeding net on the wall and a lamp hanging on a hook, casting an orange glow. Scott shifted his position for a better view and almost fell off the block in surprise when he spotted two feet in riding boots, with a thick rope knotted around the ankles. *Laura!* Twisting his neck almost full-circle like an owl, Scott made out the shadow of a man sitting in the far corner of the stable. Suddenly the man moved; there was a slurp and a glug, then a belch and a contented sigh. Carlo must be keeping himself going with a bottle of something. Something strong, Scott hoped; the drunker the guard was the better!

Steadying himself against the wall, Scott eased his phone from his jeans pocket, took a deep breath – *could this plan really work or was it the craziest idea in the history of the universe?* – and texted the word GO to Adam Martin.

Moments later he heard the mopeds buzzing in the distance like a swarm of angry wasps. The noise grew louder and louder. Horses began to neigh and the donkeys brayed as the Extreme Network tore through the stable yard and into the riding arena where they burned round and round, carving out doughnuts and pulling wheelies.

They certainly know how to cause a distraction, Scott thought.

Inside the stable, Carlo had heard it too. He was staggering to his feet and cursing under his breath in Spanish. He marched out, slamming and bolting the door behind him.

Scott prised the small window wide open. 'Laura!' he shouted. 'Up here!'

He heard a shuffling noise and soon he could see Laura's blonde hair below him.

'It's Scott. I've come to help you!' He had to yell over the roar of the mopeds.

Laura looked up. Her face was pale and streaked with tears and grime. She'd been gagged with some kind of scarf and her hands were tied in front of her with a rope that was also looped through a metal ring in the wall.

'I'm going to drop my penknife through the window. Start cutting yourself free.' Scott pulled out the blade and slid his penknife through the narrow gap. It landed on the straw with a thud. Laura was on it instantly, rolling over and grasping the knife.

Scott jumped down from the block and glanced across to the riding arena. The Extreme Network were still hurtling round in circles. Carlo – dressed in black leather jacket and jeans, and so thick-set he practically had corners – was in the middle of the ring, yelling and waving his arms, as if trying to control charging bulls in a rodeo.

Scott dashed round to the front of the stables and opened the door to find that Laura had pulled off the gag and was hacking, as best she could with her hands bound together, at the rope that tied her to the wall.

'Give me the knife.' Scott dropped to his knees and began to saw on the rope.

'Thanks!' Laura gasped, pulling the rope taut to make it easier to cut. 'That thug just leaped out of nowhere and dragged me in here. I bet he's got a bunch of buddies breaking in at the farmhouse. The Whites are out at a show in Carrickstowe.' She shook her head. 'Grr! It makes me so angry! The animals are all upset as well. I can hear them crying. And the guy's been drinking. I think he must be on some serious drugs as well because he keeps rambling on about my mum being an art forger or something. As if!' Laura hesitated and stared over Scott's shoulder. 'Er, sorry if this is a rude question, but how come you've got my mum's dog in your backpack?'

'Yeah, about that . . .' Scott began. Then he gave up. If he tried to sum up everything that had happened he'd sound as mad as Carlo. It would be like trying to fit the whole *Lord of the Rings* trilogy onto a t-shirt.

'Long story!' he said. 'I'll explain later!' There was

a ping as the last strand of the rope gave way to the penknife. Laura toppled over backwards into the straw. Scott pulled her up and, with her feet still tied together, she jumped after him to the door – just in time to hear a gunshot ring out from the riding arena.

There was a chorus of terrified neighing and braying. Wallace and Gromit were kicking and bucking in the next stable. Biscuit whimpered in the backpack.

Scott's stomach twisted in a spasm of dread. *Carlo's shot one of the Extreme Network and it's all my fault! I should never have got them involved!*

But Laura nudged him with her elbow. 'Look, he's just shooting in the air! Trying to scare off those kids on mopeds. What do they think they're *doing* shredding up the riding arena anyway? Hang on, isn't that Adam Martin and his crew?'

Scott didn't have time to reply. The boys were speeding out of the arena, crashing through the fence in their desperation to escape the flying bullets. At the same time, Carlo turned and jogged back into the yard.

'Come on!' Scott grabbed Laura's arm. 'We've got to hide!'

But it was too late.

Carlo had seen them!

Twenty

Donkey Power

'Hey!' Carlo yelled, running towards Scott and Laura, and firing the gun at random. Bullets bounced off the stable walls. And, as if things weren't bad enough already, Biscuit chose that precise moment to wriggle out of the backpack, jump to the ground and bolt into Wallace and Gromit's stable through a hole in the bottom of the door. Already freaked out by the mopeds and the gunshots, the two donkeys almost went into orbit with the arrival of a small, hyperactive dog yapping around their hooves.

Scott stood paralysed with dismay. How had everything gone so wrong? He and Laura were going be tied up and held prisoner – that's if Carlo decided to be generous and not *shoot* them both – and Biscuit was going to be trampled by crazed donkeys. There was a crash and a splinter of wood as a pair of flailing donkey hooves hit the stable door. Suddenly Scott had an idea. Maybe, just maybe, there was a way out of this train wreck!

'Stand back!' he shouted to Laura. He waited until Carlo was almost level with the Mad Donkey Stable, then dived forward, pulled back the bolt and threw the door open, jumping back just in time to avoid being mown down by the wild stampede. Carlo, however, was not so lucky. Wallace – or was it Gromit? – lowered his broad brown head, planted it firmly under the guard's belly and tossed him in the air. Carlo crash-landed on his back with a *whump*! He was trying to push himself up on his elbows when a flying hoof caught him on the kneecap.

'Aaaaghh!' he cried, clutching his leg, winded and crippled.

Biscuit trotted out of the stable, seemingly unruffled by his brush with the hooves of doom.

Scott punched the air, as much with relief as victory. 'Donkey power!' He turned to Laura. 'We need to tie Carlo up.'

But Laura was one step ahead. She'd already snagged a rope with a loop in the end from the donkeys' stable. She took aim but at the last moment Carlo rolled to the side and dodged the lasso.

'Drat!' Laura muttered, trying to gather the rope for another throw. 'I can't do this with my hands tied up.'

'Let me!' Scott grabbed the rope and tossed it. He was as astonished as Carlo when the loop dropped perfectly over his head and shoulders.

'Pull to tighten it up!' Laura shouted.

Scott yanked the rope tight. Carlo thrashed around like a landed fish, swearing and snarling, but his arms were pinned to his sides and every time he tried to get to his feet, his donkey-trodden knee gave way.

'Hey! You'd make a good cowboy!' Laura told Scott.

Scott grinned. If only Jack could have seen that cool lasso throw. He wished he had it on video! He took his penknife and started cutting the ropes from Laura's ankles and wrists.

Suddenly the mopeds were roaring back into the yard.

'Hey, what were you lot doing pulling those stunts in my riding arena?' Laura shouted. 'You've trashed it!'

Still sitting astride his bike, Adam held up his hands. 'Whoah! What about *Thanks, guys, for helping with the rescue plan*? Or *Thanks, guys, for saving my life*?'

Laura looked at Scott with a baffled expression.

'It's true,' Scott explained. 'I asked them to provide

153

a distraction to get Carlo out of the way.' He turned to Adam and held up his hand for a high-five. 'Great work, guys!'

'Hang on a minute,' Laura interrupted. 'How come you all knew I'd been taken prisoner in the first place?'

Scott took a deep breath. He'd been dreading having to tell Laura what was going on, but she had to find out some time. 'What Carlo told you was true. Your mum *was* involved with an art theft gang in the past. And now she's in danger,' he added seriously. 'Carlo's boss has taken her to the Trago Gallery.'

Laura stared at him for a long moment. Just when Scott thought the shock had blown a fuse in her brain, she snapped back to her senses. 'We've got to get up there and rescue her!' she cried, kicking the last of the ropes off her riding boots. All of a sudden Laura was taking charge. 'You guys!' she instructed Adam Martin. 'Tie Carlo up properly and stand guard. And you can call the police and tell them there's a robbery in progress at the Trago Gallery.' Then she turned to Scott. 'Can you ride?'

'*Ride?*' Scott echoed. This seemed a strange time for a riding lesson!

'Yeah, can you ride a horse? It's the quickest way to the gallery. We can gallop cross-country to the headland!'

Scott gulped. He'd been pony trekking on an activity week in Wales when he was in Year Six. But that involved sitting on a pony while it pottered around in the woods. There had been no mention of *galloping*. 'Yeah, I can ride!' Scott couldn't believe he'd said that out loud. Was he turning into Jack or what? Next he'd be saying, *How hard can it be?*

Laura smiled. 'I'll saddle up Peppercorn for you. He's nice and steady.'

'Great!' Scott tried to sound slightly less terrified than he felt.

While Laura was getting the ponies ready Scott checked his phone. Still no call from Emily to say how they'd got on with swapping the paintings at the gallery. He quickly sent her a text to tell her Laura was safe and they were on their way.

Laura led out a little black pony and handed Scott the reins. Then she swung herself up into the saddle of her own horse, a dapple grey with flowing white mane. 'Put Biscuit in the backpack and let me take him,' she said. 'He'll throw you off balance.'

Scott zipped the little dog back inside and passed the backpack up to Laura, then buckled on the helmet she'd handed him and put his foot in the stirrup. Grasping the saddle as he'd seen Laura do, he propelled himself upwards with all the strength he could muster. *Too much strength,* it seemed; he sailed over the top of the pony and landed on the other side, flat out on the concrete yard floor.

There was a round of applause from the Extreme

Network. 'Cool move, Scotto!' they laughed. They'd already tied Carlo up so well that he looked like an Egyptian mummy and were now running around with the lasso trying to recapture Wallace and Gromit.

On the second attempt Scott managed to make contact with the saddle, and moments later he was hanging on for his life as Peppercorn accelerated out of the yard faster than a souped-up Ferrari. They were galloping along, following Laura on her white charger, hooves pounding, wind rushing past, hair and mane flying. Instinctively, Scott leaned forward as they sailed over hedges and ditches, across the fields and the moors beyond.

It was the most thrillingly insane experience of his life.

But would they be in time to rescue Mrs Roberts from Delgado's clutches?

And what kind of trouble had Jack and Emily got themselves into?

Twenty-one

Stupid Heroics

There was a *thwump*, a startled cry and then silence.

Emily could hardly bear to look out from behind the grizzly bear. When she did, she saw Jack spread-eagled on top of Delgado in the hall below. They looked as if they'd both been run over by a cartoon steamroller. She hugged Drift to her chest and buried her face in his fur. *I should have known he'd do something mad like this!*

157

Stupid heroics, Scott called it. *I should have stopped him. What if he's . . .*

Emily forced herself to peep out through her fingers and take another look. A wave of relief crashed over her. Delgado and Jack were both now moving. Delgado was writhing around trying to dislodge Jack from his back. But Jack sat up and pressed Delgado's shoulders to the tiles with his hands. He grinned triumphantly as if he'd just won a wrestling bout with Hulk Hogan. *But has Jack's Ninja leap flattened Delgado in time?* Emily wondered. *Has Delgado pressed that key on his phone to signal Laura's death?*

Suddenly everyone was moving at once. Mrs Roberts darted forward to pick up Delgado's phone, which had flown out of his hand when Jack landed on top of him. The police officers ran across to handcuff Delgado. D.I. Hassan glanced up to the staircase to see where the Flying Boy had sprung from. But everyone stopped and turned to stare as the front door flew open.

For a moment Emily thought she was seeing things! But no, it really *was* Laura Roberts!

Laura ran into the hall, followed by Scott – who, for some reason Emily couldn't figure out – was wearing a riding helmet.

'Mum!' Laura shouted.

'Laura!' Mrs Roberts sobbed, dropping Delgado's phone.

Laura threw herself into her mother's arms.

'And you've got Biscuit too!' Mrs Roberts laughed, taking him out of the backpack and hugging him as well. The little white dog wagged his stumpy tail and licked the tears of joy from Mrs Roberts' face.

Emily snuggled Drift on her lap. She was crying with happiness too!

Meanwhile Jack was getting to his feet. 'He's all yours!' he said to the police officers – in his best super-cool James Bond voice.

Delgado sat up and looked around. Jack flashed him a pleasant smile, but Delgado scrunched his eyebrows into a thunderous scowl.

Understandable, Jack thought. Things were definitely not going to plan today for Juan Delgado! Bianca had nicked his priceless masterpiece off him at gunpoint, he'd been squashed by a flying power-slam and handcuffed by the police. And now his hostage – the only bargaining tool he had left – had just marched in through the front door!

Scott wobbled slowly towards Jack. After the death-defying gallop across the moors his legs were so shaky he felt as if he was walking on a bouncy castle. He almost keeled over when two more police officers came barrelling in through a side door.

'Sorry, Chief,' one of them puffed to D.I. Hassan. 'We lost her! Must have climbed out through a window. Who was she, anyway?'

'That was Bianca Mendez, alias Nina Rodriguez of

159

the Copycat Gang.' Everyone looked up to see Emily coming down the stairs with Drift at her side. She walked across the hall and stood next to Jack and Scott. 'She's stolen Digory Trago's *Animal Orchestra* and now she'll be climbing down the cliff. She was out preparing the route last night.'

'Never mind the Trago painting!' Delgado spat. 'She's got da Vinci's *Lady in Blue!*'

D. I. Hassan regarded him coolly, smoothing his luxuriant black moustache with his thumb and forefinger. 'The *Lady in Blue* was stolen from the National Gallery back in the eighties,' he chuckled. 'Pull the other one! How on earth would it have found its way here?'

Long story, Scott thought.

'It's true,' Mrs Roberts said. 'I hid it here. But Delgado's right. Nina has taken it.'

Jack stepped forward. He'd been waiting for his Big Moment and he was going to make the most of it. 'But no!' he proclaimed dramatically, taking the rolled-up canvas that Emily passed to him and holding it aloft like the Olympic torch. 'The painting you took from the mouth of the flying pig, and that Bianca – or Nina or whatever her name is – has scarpered with, is *not* the original. *This* is!' Jack unfurled the scroll and basked in glory as everyone stared in stunned silence at the real *Lady in Blue.*

'But how?' Mrs Roberts spluttered. 'I saw . . .'

'We switched the real painting for the print from your

house just a few moments before you and Delgado got here tonight,' Emily explained.

'What? The one I got Mum from Carrickstowe?' Laura asked.

Poor Laura! Jack thought. He'd never seen anyone look so bewildered – not even in a maths lesson when the teacher mentioned quadratic equations.

D. I. Hassan held out his hands for the painting. 'I think we'll let the experts have a look at this. In the meantime, let's get these two back to the police station.' He gestured for the police officers to take Delgado and Mrs Roberts away. 'There are a *lot* of questions that need answering.'

'I'd better get the ponies back to the stables,' Laura mumbled, hurrying away, followed by a policewoman who offered to go with her.

'We'll just be getting back home then,' Jack mumbled, pulling Emily and Scott towards the door. With luck they could slip away before D. I. Hassan decided he had questions for *them* too. But they weren't quite quick enough.

'And I'll have even *more* questions for you three in the morning.' D. I. Hassan's booming voice followed them out into the night.

The three friends and Drift ran to the back of the building where Emily and Jack had left their bikes. It was now dark and a half-moon was rising. They collapsed onto a bank of soft, springy grass, all talking at the same time, laughing and high-fiving at the success of Operation Copycat. Drift bounced happily among them. He had no idea what was going on but you could never have too much rolling around in the grass in his book!

'That secret entrance is awesome!' Jack laughed, pointing out the balcony to Scott. 'You've got to try it!'

'I think I'll take a rain check on that,' Scott said. 'That rescue mission has worn me out!'

'Where's your bike, Scott?' Emily asked, sitting up. 'How did you get here?'

'Horseback!' Scott replied.

'On a *horse*?' Jack snorted, as if Scott was claiming to have travelled by magic broomstick. 'But you can't ride!'

Scott grinned. 'Apparently I can!'

Jack laughed and rapped on Scott's riding helmet with his knuckles. 'Well, I guess that explains the comedy headgear!'

Scott had forgotten he was still wearing the riding hat. He quickly took it off and shook his head to get rid of a bad case of helmet-hair.

'So *you've* been pulling off some stupid heroics too?' Emily asked.

Scott thought for a moment. Fighting off an armed guard with nothing but a pair of psycho donkeys and a lasso – yeah, that was all firmly in stupid heroics territory. He grinned and shrugged.

'You two are as bad as each other!' Emily laughed.

'You missed Jack leaping off the banister onto Delgado.'

'Like a black panther pouncing on an antelope, wasn't I?' Jack said.

'Yeah, something like that!' Emily giggled. 'Of course,' she added, poking Jack in the side, 'if it wasn't for me, you'd still be wandering around talking to yourself in the mirror!'

'And if it wasn't for *Drift,* we'd never have heard Delgado coming and hidden behind the bear in time,' Jack added, hastily changing the subject. 'Way to go, Drifty!'

Drift sat up and looked pleased with himself.

'So, that's Operation Copycat done and dusted,' Scott said, getting to his feet. 'I hope Mrs Roberts doesn't get sent to prison.'

Jack stood up too. 'Surely they'll let her off after all these years of good behaviour? She *was* going to give the *Lady in Blue* back, after all.'

'Yes, and we can prove it,' Emily said. 'We'll show D.I. Hassan that letter she wrote for us to give to the police tomorrow.' She glanced at her watch. 'Oh, no! It's late! If I don't get home I'll definitely be grounded this time!' She jumped on her bike. Drift hopped into his basket and they took off down the hill. 'See you tomorrow!' she called over her shoulder.

'See you tomorrow!' Jack and Scott called back. They stood for a moment watching the lights of the police cars driving down the winding road, past the ice works towards the village. A silver path of moonlight sparkled across the bay. Silhouetted against the moonlight, the two ponies were being led down the path across the headland. In the distance, Scott heard the buzz of mopeds.

'That'll be Adam Martin and the Extreme Network,' he said. 'I'm a member now, by the way. I'll tell you about it on the way home.'

Jack grinned. 'Remember when we thought nothing ever happened in Castle Key?'

Scott laughed. 'Yeah! Dead boring!'

Jack pulled his bike out from under a gorse bush. 'Do you want a lift on the back?' he asked. 'We could really get some speed up down that hill!'

Author's Note

You've probably heard of Leonardo da Vinci's famous portrait, the Mona Lisa, *but don't worry if you've never heard of the* Lady in Blue. *It was invented for the purposes of this mystery. Da Vinci never painted a portrait of this name . . . as far as we know!*

Don't miss the next exciting mystery
in the *Adventure Island* series

THE MYSTERY OF THE
CURSED RUBY

Available September 2011!

Read on for a special preview of the first chapter.

One

The Circus Comes to Town

'The circus starts tonight. We've got to go!'

Emily Wild scrambled up onto the sun-baked rocks and sat hugging her little dog Drift and gazing out over Pirate Cove. The Romaldi Circus always came to Castle Key for the last week of the summer holidays and Emily had gone every year she could remember. This year the theme of the show was the Arabian Nights. She couldn't wait!

But Scott wasn't exactly jumping up and down with excitement. He'd noticed the circus setting up on the common, of course. You could hardly *miss* a convoy of trucks and caravans and a red-and-yellow-striped big top. Especially when it was only a few minutes away from Stone Cottage, where he and Jack were staying for the summer with their Great-aunt Kate. But weren't circuses a bit on the *cheesy* side? Clowns with silly shoes and red noses squirting each other with water? That sounded right up there at the gorgonzola end of the cheesiness scale.

His younger brother Jack was more enthusiastic. 'I'm up for it!' he said, rummaging through the picnic bag for a packet of crisps. 'As long as there's a lion-tamer with *really* ferocious lions. Oh, and some tigers.'

'Jack Carter!' Emily cried, aiming a sandwich crust at his head. 'They don't have animals, apart from a horse and a poodle. Making wild animals perform tricks would be cruel!'

'Yeah, *obviously*! I was joking!' Jack said, back-tracking rapidly. 'What *do* they have then?'

'Oh, acrobats, sword-swallowers, flying trapeze . . . It's *amazing!*'

'Sword-swallowers?' Jack echoed. '*Now* you're talking!' He threw back his head, and did a revoltingly realistic sword-swallowing mime using the last crisp. 'Anyone fancy another swim?'

Drift pricked up his ears, the black one and the white

one with brown spots. *Swim* was one of his favourite words!

Scott stretched and pretended he wasn't interested. Then he leaped up and took off across the scorching sand towards the waves. 'Last one in buys the circus tickets!' he shouted over his shoulder.

———

Scott had to admit Emily was right. Sitting in the front row of the packed big top, he couldn't help being seriously impressed by the Romaldi Circus. The show opened with a dramatic laser light display and swirling Arabian music. Suddenly they were plunged into darkness. Stars gradually twinkled into life all over the roof of the big top. Flying carpets began swooping in from every direction and hovering above the circus ring. The performers hopped down from the carpets, backflipping and cartwheeling around the ring in a welcome parade. And that was just the opening sequence.

Sitting between Scott and Jack, with Drift curled up on her lap, Emily joined in the applause. But beneath the excitement, she couldn't help feeling a trace of sadness. Coming to the circus meant the summer holidays were almost over. And what a summer it had been – full of secret passages, flooded caves, ghosts, film stars, buried treasure and stolen masterpieces. But soon Scott and Jack's dad would be back from his archaeological dig in Africa. The boys would be going home to London. School loomed just over the horizon. Emily didn't *mind* school in principle but it took up valuable time she'd much rather spend conducting important investigations.

Emily jumped as Jack nudged her arm and shook a bag of popcorn under her nose. She snapped back to reality and settled down to enjoy the show. The ringmaster was galloping around on a magnificent white horse. Enzo Romaldi – a stern-looking old man with bushy white eyebrows and moustache – was dressed as a sultan in a fabulous jewelled turban and cloak. He pulled the horse up in the middle of the ring and introduced the first act. '. . . the Sword of Persia, a man who laughs in the face of peril . . .'

Jack craned forward in his seat. 'Sounds like my kind of guy!'

Accompanied by the beating of gongs, a huge copper-coloured man burst into the ring, juggling six mighty scimitars, their blades flashing in the spotlights. He was wearing leggings and wrist-guards of tooled leather and a metal breastplate. His back was tattooed with crossed swords. To Jack's delight, the Sword of Persia wasn't content with just *swallowing* swords; he set them alight and *then* swallowed three of them, while hanging upside-down over a bed of nails.

'Don't try this at home!' Emily whispered to Jack.

'Spoilsport!' Jack brandished his stick of candy-floss like a flaming sword.

Scott shook his head. 'I'm telling Aunt Kate to lock the cutlery drawer!'

For his next trick, the Sword inserted six long swords into a giant Ali Baba jar. He tipped the jar over to show the audience how the blades criss-crossed inside. Then he removed the swords and his assistant – a lady in a belly-dancing outfit – climbed inside. She smiled and waved as the Sword of Persia placed the lid on the jar. Slowly, he slid the swords into the jar again, jiggling each one a little until the tip poked out through a small hole on the other side.

Emily cringed. She could almost *feel* the cold metal blades on her skin. Of course, she knew the lady wasn't *really* being stabbed. There had to be a trick to that jar. She wished she could get inside and see how it worked. At last, the Sword of Persia drew the swords out and sliced the air with a flourish and a cry of *Open Sesame*! The assistant jumped out and belly-danced around the ring – not a puncture wound in sight.

'How did they do that?' Jack marvelled. 'I thought she'd be skewered like a kebab.'

'False bottom!' Scott said knowledgeably.

'I dunno. It looks real to me!' Jack laughed, glancing at the belly-dancer's wiggling hips.

The Sword of Persia was followed by acrobats and jugglers and a contortionist who folded herself up inside tiny boxes and bags. There was an incredible mind-reading act called Incognito. He was a sinister figure, in lizard-green body paint and a long black cloak, who appeared like a genie from a giant golden lamp in Aladdin's cave, and could somehow guess people's secret wishes. Then Mimi the poodle took to the ring. Her trainer played the part of the bored Princess Jasmine, locked in a tower. Mimi – her fur dyed pale pink and sporting a veil and jewelled headband – pulled off amazing balancing tricks to fetch beautiful objects to amuse the princess.

'I thought *you* were the smartest dog in town, Drift,' Scott joked, 'but I bet you couldn't do that.'

'He could if he *wanted* to!' Emily said loyally. 'But how often is he going to need to walk backwards along a tightrope?'

Drift's ears pricked up as he watched. But whether he was more interested in Mimi's sensational sense of balance or her cute little pom-pom tail, it was hard to tell.

The grand finale was the trapeze act. The Flying Romaldis' breathtaking display told a story of young princesses who turned into birds to escape from their palace, and were then pursued by evil guards. Emily watched in amazement as a girl – not much older than she was – swan-dived from the very pinnacle of the big top. Just as it seemed she would free-fall into the audience, one of the men caught her and tossed her back up into the air to land on a tiny platform.

'Wow!' Scott said. 'These guys are good!'

'Good?' Jack laughed. 'They're awesome!' Spellbound, he watched as the girl swooped overhead again. She let go of the swing, caught it with her feet, then sprang backwards; one flip, two flips and here was the guy flying in to catch her again as she soared past. She reached for his outstretched arms but at the last moment he seemed to draw back. The girl lunged for his wrists again and then grabbed at an empty trapeze. But it was too late.

The entire audience gasped.

Then there was a terrible silence as the girl spun out over the edge of the safety net and plummeted to the ground.